T0247365

FISH SOUP

CHARCO  PRESS

First published by Charco Press 2018

Charco Press Ltd., Office 59, 44-46 Morningside Road, Edinburgh EH10 4BF

ISBN: 978 1 9998593 0 5

e-book: 978 1 9998593 5 0

www.charcopress.com

Edited by Fionn Petch

Cover design by Pablo Font

Typeset by Laura Jones

2   4   6   8   10   9   7   5   3

LOTTERY FUNDED

Margarita García Robayo

FISH SOUP

Translated by
Charlotte Coombe

CHARCO PRESS

I am writing these poems
From inside a lion,
And it's rather dark in here.
So please excuse the handwriting
Which may not be too clear.

Shel Silverstein, *It's Dark in Here*

PART I

WAITING FOR A HURRICANE

1

Living by the sea is both good and bad for exactly the same reason: the world ends at the horizon. That is, the world never ends. And you always expect too much. At first, you hope everything you're waiting for will arrive one day on a boat; then you realise nothing's going to arrive and you'll have to go looking for it instead. I hated my city because it was both really beautiful and really ugly, and I was somewhere in the middle. The middle was the worst place to be: hardly anyone made it out of the middle. It was where the lost causes lived: there, nobody was poor enough to resign themselves to being poor forever, so they spent their lives trying to move up in the world and liberate themselves. When all attempts failed – as they usually did – their self-awareness disappeared and that's when all was lost. My family, for example, had no self-awareness whatsoever. They'd found ways of fleeing reality, of seeing things from a long way off, looking down on it all from their castle in the sky. And most of the time, it worked.

My father was a pretty useless man. He spent his days trying to resolve trivial matters that he thought were of the utmost importance in order for the world to keep on turning. Things like getting the most out of the pair of taxis we owned and making sure the drivers weren't stealing from him. But they were always stealing from him. His friend Felix, who drove a van for a chemist, always came griping to him: I saw that waste-of-space who drives your taxi out and about… Where? On Santander Avenue, burning rubber with some little whore. My dad fired and hired drivers every day as a matter of course and this helped him, 1) to feel powerful, and 2) not to think about anything else.

My mother also kept herself occupied, but with other things: every day she was involved in some family bust-up. Every day, that was her formula. As soon as my mother got out of bed she would pick up the phone, call my aunt, or my uncle, or my other aunt, and she shouted and cried and wished them dead; them and their damned mother, who was also her mother, my grandmother. Sometimes she also called my grandmother, and shouted and cried and wished her dead too, her and her damned offspring. My mother loved saying the word "damned", she found it cathartic and liberating; although she would never have expressed it that way because she had a limited vocabulary. The third call of the day was to Don Hector, who she always sucked up to because he let her buy things on tick: Good morning, Don Hector, how are you? Could you send me a loaf of bread and half a dozen eggs? Her face awash with tears. Her formula was the same as my father's: making sure that there were no lulls, no dead time that might cause them to look around and realise where they were: in a tiny apartment in a second-rate neighbourhood, with a sewer pipe and various bus routes running through it.

I was not like them, I very quickly realised where I was, and at the age of seven I already knew that I would leave. I didn't know when, or where I would go. When people asked me, what do you want to be when you grow up? I'd reply: a foreigner. My brother also knew that he wanted to get out of there, and he made the decisions he needed to achieve this: he quit high school to devote all his time to working out at the gym and making out with *gringas* he met on the beach. Because, for him, leaving meant someone taking him away. He wanted to live either in Miami or New York, he was undecided. He studied English because it would be useful in either city. Less so in Miami, that's what his friend Rafa told him. Rafa had been out of the country once, when he was very young. I liked Rafa because he had got out, and that was something to be admired. But then I met Gustavo, who had not left but arrived, and not from one country, but several.

Gustavo. Gustavo was a man who lived in a house in front of the sea. More of a shack, really. Outside the shack there was a shelter propped up with four poles and a tarpaulin roof. Under the shelter, there was a worktable with a long bench, a double wooden seat, a hammock. My father used to go and buy fish from him on Sundays, and sometimes he took me with him. As well as fish, Gustavo had a pool full of enormous shellfish that he bred himself: crabs, lobsters, even sea snakes. He was Argentinian, or Italian, depending on the day. The first time my father took me to his shack (I must have been about twelve), Gustavo said to me: Do you want me to teach you how to descale them? To do what? To clean the fish. He was sitting on a step at the edge of the pool with his legs spread wide, a washing-up bowl full of fish on the ground next to him. A second bowl was for putting the clean fish in. I imitated the way he sat, but in front, with my back to him. He held my hands and showed me how to do it. Then he stroked me down there with two fingers: up and down, up and down, he said, while I cleaned the fish with a sharpened machete and he traced a vertical line on my magic button – that's what my mother's friend Charo used to call it, when she wanted to tell her some gossip that involved the word "pussy", and I was within earshot. While Gustavo was doing that, my father was laying out some notes on the table: for fish guts and bellies, wrapped in newspaper, to make oil. Did you see what Gustavo did? I asked him when we were back in the taxi, on the way home. My father was driving slowly, a bolero by Alci Acosta was playing on the radio. He taught you how to clean the fish, he said. Yes, but, he also… He also what? Never mind. And after that I carried on going to Gustavo's house, sometimes on my own, sometimes with my father, sometimes after school, sometimes instead of school.

I liked the sound of the waves…

Gustavo, will you take me to Italy? What for? To live. No. What about Argentina? What for? Same thing. No.

Then, his fingers.

2

One day, I went to school, waited for them to take the register and then left. I used to do this with Maritza Caballero, a friend who didn't live there anymore because her dad, who was a soldier in the Marines, had been posted to Medellín. I didn't understand what she was going to do in Medellín, which was all mountains. The soldiers lived in Manzanillo, a gated community at the edge of the bay, in prefab houses that smelled of damp because of the humidity there.

Water and wood are not good friends, that's what Maritza would say about her house.

So that day they took the register and I left, but without Maritza. I left school at quarter to eight, I was hungry and didn't have much money. I wandered around the city centre for a while. It was full of people hurrying to work at the law courts or going to sit in Plaza Bolívar to read the newspaper. I sat down in the square and was bored.

When Maritza was there, we used to sit on the city wall to look at the avenue, the boardwalk, and beyond that, the sea. She wanted to be a lawyer and work in the courts; I told her I did too, but that was a lie. I didn't want to be anything. Maritza said that I could be anything I wanted, because I did well at school. Maritza would look me straight in the eyes when she talked, which made me uneasy: she had yellow hair and yellow eyes and very pale skin. She was the most washed-out person I knew.

I was one chromosome away from being an albino, that's what Maritza used to say about herself.

But she was beautiful, especially at night, because in the daytime, in the sunlight, her veins were really visible.

I caught a bus to Gustavo's house and found him with a far-away look in his eye. When I found him like this, it was because he had an easy order to deliver that day. For a lobster, all he had to do, for example, was reach into the pool and grab one when he needed it.

Make me a little prawn cocktail, I said, handing him the bag of limes I had picked up at a fruit stall by the road, before I got on the bus. It was only then that he turned to look at me, squinted and said: this morning, there was a cold draught of air coming through the crack under the door and running up my legs. Oh? And he went on talking: that made me get out of bed. I had a rum to warm myself up and chewed on a piece of old bread that was so hard it practically broke my jaw. What did you do then? Then I went fishing, but I didn't catch anything, the sea was too choppy. Mm-hm.

It was nine thirty.

Gustavo peeled some prawns and told me to fetch some onion, mayonnaise and chilli from the kitchen. The kitchen in that shack was filthy, the whole shack was filthy, and I hated going inside.

I told him I didn't want a prawn cocktail after all. What? I don't want any-fucking-thing now. He replied: I'll wash that mouth of yours out with bleach. So I went to get what was needed and Gustavo made me a delicious cocktail, I wolfed it down in one go. I sipped the pink juice at the bottom of the glass, and it tasted spicy. Wake me up at one, I told him, and went to sleep in the hammock.

Another day I did the same thing, but I didn't bring any limes, so I went straight to the hammock to have a snooze. Gustavo didn't pay me much attention as he was busy peeling a mountain of prawns, which he was putting into a Styrofoam cool box filled with ice. In the evening he had to deliver several kilos for a big *quinceañera* party.

Wake me up at one, I told him, and shut my eyes.

It took me a while to fall asleep: it was hot, it smelled of salt, my skin felt clammy.

When I opened my eyes, they met Gustavo's.

What are you doing? Nothing. He was studying me, sitting on a stool in front of the hammock. The sun streamed in through one side of the roof where the tarpaulin was ripped, and it illuminated part of his face. I told him he was going to get burned just on one side, like a carnival mask. My brother had a carnival mask he had bought in Barranquilla. "Night and day", it was called. I used to put it on sometimes, but it was too big for me. Gustavo got up off the stool and went back to his prawns. Is it one yet? No. What time is it? Half past eleven.

The next time I opened my eyes, Gustavo wasn't there. The mountain of prawns was on the table and there was a four-door pick-up truck parked on the beach. I sat up in the hammock and looked at the sea: a boat, a man with a net in the distance. Somewhere a dog was barking.

After a while, Gustavo got out of the pick-up truck, adjusting his shorts. Behind him, a lady got out, rearranging her hair. Gustavo picked up the cooler and carried it to the pickup truck. The lady said to me: have you turned fifteen yet? No. Good. Why? Her: because lately, nobody splashes out on *quinceañeras* anymore. If it's a buffet, they don't serve seafood, forget it; and if it's a sit-down affair, not even a whiff. And what do they serve? They serve rice and chicken and potato salad packed full of onion, so that when the girls go and chat to the boys afterwards, they have dogshit breath. But not Melissa. Melissa's going to have a party the way a *quinceañera* party should be.

Melissa?

Gustavo came back. The lady pulled out some notes that were tucked inside her bra and gave them to him. I'm going to serve them with tartar sauce, she said, what do you think of tartar sauce? He put the notes down on the table. I thought they might blow away.

It makes me want to puke, I said.

3

There was a time when the weather completely changed. It rained all the time, every day it rained. That was bad for the ground because it got eroded; bad for the sea, because it got rough; bad for the TV because it got no signal. We still had the radio. The radio said that the city was going through a tragic situation; not in the modern parts, where the rich people lived, but in the shantytowns around the banks of the Ciénaga de la Virgen lagoon. Because it was full of crap, it overflowed, and the flimsy houses sank into the mud. It was around that time that people started talking about the Submarine Outfall, a metal pipe that would swallow all the shit built up in the Ciénaga, carry it out to sea and spew it out. It was the solution to all the city's problems. They hadn't built it yet because there was no money, and there was no money because it had been stolen. Who by? Nobody knew. On the radio everyone was talking about it. After that came the romantic programmes, playing a top ten of songs about rain.

One day during that time, I dreamed that the wind carried off my brother and his friend Julián, who he used to go to the gym with. They were whisked away, clinging to one another, their teeth gritted like when they flexed their muscles in front of the mirror. I watched them float higher and higher until I couldn't see them anymore. Another day, I dreamed that the wind blew away Willy's kiosk: he sold beers near Gustavo's shack. Willy hated me because one day

I kicked a pig in the head as it was snuffling around my feet. The pig ran off, terrified and squealing like an old woman, and I laughed. Willy got angry: you're evil, he told me. And I told him he was a black bastard. Gustavo grabbed me by the wrist and twisted my arm. I wrenched myself free and ran off. I didn't go back for months.

We had arrived at the kiosk half an hour before that, after a long walk on the beach. I'd been talking to Gustavo about Maritza Caballero, who'd sent me a postcard from Medellín, and a photo of her in the mountains; she was wearing a blue hoodie. I'd never worn a hoodie. I was thirsty, and Gustavo said, let's go to Willy's kiosk. He ordered an Águila beer for him, and a Coca-Cola for me. We sat on stools at the counter, and Willy started talking about a cruise ship full of *gringos* that had just come in. He said he was waiting for Brígida, the black fruit-seller who wore bright dresses. They were going to town to flog things to the *gringos*: beer, rum, shell necklaces. Got any oysters, boss? Willy only called Gustavo "boss" because he was white and a foreigner. Gustavo never tipped him, and even spat on the ground sometimes, but Willy still called him "boss". That day, however, a black fisherman turned up, ordered a beer and after the first sip, let out a huge belch. Willy said to him: didn't your mother teach you any manners, you black bastard?

The rain was also bad for my family, because the sewer pipe near our house overflowed, the pavements turned green and the air stank to high heaven. My dad lost a taxi: it filled up with water, right up to the engine, and had to be scrapped. That time, he sat everyone down around the table and declared: now we are poor, and started to cry like a little child. I looked around: my brother was checking his watch impatiently, because he was supposed to be going to the cinema with Julián and two women from Bogotá they had picked up at La Escollera. My mother was folding handkerchiefs, deep in concentration. Next to her was a wicker basket full of faded underpants and a load of single socks tangled up in a ball.

Being poor was exactly the same as not being poor. There was nothing to worry about.

4

When I left school, I enrolled in a law degree. It was a public university but there was an enrolment fee to pay, which was based on the income of your father. In my case, it was a tiny fee, but my father said to me: hopefully you'll get a scholarship, so you can carry on. But I don't want to carry on, I replied. Of course you do, he said, and winked at me. One day a girl in my class told me: they're giving out visas to go and live in Canada. I went to the consulate to find out. You had to know English and French, and they were giving priority to young professional couples, with plans to procreate. My friend told me that in Canada they were running out of young people, and that this was their plan to repopulate the country. Repopulate it with Latinos? Better than nothing, she said. But I was a long way from being a young professional with a husband and plans to procreate. Canada would not be my destiny. I didn't even like Canada: not a single film actor was from Canada. There was nothing in Canada, apart from old people.

In those days, the baby belonging to the maid Xenaida used to cry all night long.

She'd got knocked up, nobody knew who by. My brother accused the janitor. But she gave nothing away. When she told my mother about the pregnancy, my mother fired her and Xenaida got down on her knees and begged: *señora*, just let me have the baby and then I'll go. Now she'd given birth to the baby, and she was still here.

13

The baby cried like it was possessed.

One night my brother went into her room and shook her by the shoulders: Xenaida! She was fast asleep, dead to the world. The tiny wrinkled baby was screaming its lungs out on the floor, on top of a pile of clothes, its arms and legs flailing around, like a turtle stranded on its back. Xenaida used to put him there so he wouldn't fall off the bed.

Gustavo. What? Is Olga your girlfriend? No.

Gustavo was seeing a woman called Olga.

Foreigners like black women, my mother used to say.

Olga swept the shack and wore a thin, dirty dress. Olga would put her hands down the front of her dress to hoik up her breasts, and that made me nervous. Olga didn't understand what I was always doing there, and she didn't like it: next time you come sniffing around I'll slash your face with the machete. Gustavo heard her but would say nothing. Once, Olga heated up a banana with the skin on and everything, then she sat down on a stool, lifted her skirt and put it right inside her. Her eyes rolled back in her head. Gustavo and I saw her from the worktable: he was filleting a sea bass, I was descaling a tarpon. The sea was calm, the sun burning bright.

That's when Gustavo began telling his stories. This was the first story Gustavo told me:

When I was young, I had a motorbike and lots of hair on my head. I had blond hair, before it turned white and straggly. It was impossible to drag a comb through it, but some of my girlfriends insisted on brushing it for me. That would really piss me off. And when I got pissed off, I'd get on my bike and go far away.

Far away from what?

I finished my first year of law and I was awarded the scholarship. It was easy to get it, I reckon I could've got any scholarship I wanted. But I said that I didn't want any scholarship, that what I wanted was to go far away. But where? the professor of Roman Law asked me, taken aback. I shrugged. He had gone away once, but had come back, he told me. Why? Because I missed it. What did you miss? The food, the culture. I hardly ate anything and didn't give a shit about culture. I shook the teacher's hand, then turned my back on him and left. Left his class, and everything else, and started going to the gym with my brother.

Gustavo. What? Do you think I'm pretty? Yes. Do you want me to take off my clothes? No. Gustavo. What? Don't you like me anymore? Don't you have some legal code you're supposed to be reading? I've already read them all. Well, in that case I'll tell you a story.

We lay down in the hammock, but Gustavo would no longer touch my magic button. Instead, he stroked my head. One day, I asked him to. But why do you want me to do that? he asked. Because you did it before. And he said that he didn't like it, that it wasn't fun anymore. I thought he did like it, but it was Olga who didn't. Olga would come and hang around occasionally, using any excuse. But eventually she left: she rolled her eyes at me and left. And Gustavo said:

Once upon a time there was a ship that set sail from Corsica, destination unknown, and halfway through the voyage, most of the crew died.

If the destination was unknown, how did they know they were halfway through the voyage?

…some, the youngest, died of hunger; others died of disease, and others just died. They threw the dead overboard. They threw my mother into the sea, and my little sister Niní.

Was she really called Niní, or was that her nickname?

…those of us who survived reached a vast, lush, green country. We ate whole cows, raw.

I hate raw things, I like things medium rare.

...part of the meat would always go bad, because the cows were as big as hippopotamuses, and I used to think how much my mother and Niní would have loved that country. So green, so big, so full of fat raw cows.

...sushi, for example, I can't stand it.

It was the best country in the world, but I couldn't live there because it reminded me too much of the dead bodies we'd thrown into the sea. Of my mother and Niní. That's why I left. First to Peru, then to Ecuador and so on up, until I reached the Caribbean, where you turn left to carry on north. But then I built this shack, and I decided to stay.

And when do I appear?

I didn't appear in Gustavo's story.

In December, a strong wind swept away the houses in one of the poorer neighbourhoods, and they held a telethon for the victims. In December, Xenaida got sepsis, because of a botched C-section. It was two months since she'd given birth, the wound was already getting infected, and she hadn't told anyone. They took her to a hospital and my mother was left to take care of the baby: he cried and cried and cried. After a week in hospital, Xenaida died. It was nearly Christmas. My mother called an aunt of Xenaida's in a small village, but she had died too. There was nobody to take care of the wailing baby. Social Services said they would come and get him, but they didn't. It was a very busy time, they said later, when my mother took him there herself. She handed him over, like a filthy little bundle, to a woman with glasses who pursed her lips as soon as she saw him. Hmm, he's very skinny, but potbellied too, he must have worms.

5

One day, I fell in love. His name was Antonio, but everyone called him Tony. I called him sweetheart, and he called me sweetheart. Tony had a motorbike and he used to take me out on it; then we'd go to the beach, a beach far away, where only fishermen went. A beach with black sand, not like the ones you see in the movies. I had a towel in my gym bag, and I would shake it out and lay it on the sand. Tony also went to the gym and wanted to be an architect, he said, as we watched a sailboat almost touching the horizon, bobbing along like it was drunk. Drunk on champagne. I wanted a sailboat too, but only rich people had sailboats. Only rich people drank champagne.

Then I said to Tony: if I was rich I wouldn't want to leave, rich people can live well anywhere; I wouldn't care about the heat or the black sand or the watery lentils my mother cooks. And Tony said: if you were rich, your mother wouldn't cook watery lentils. What would she cook? Caviar. You don't cook caviar. Whatever; that's what you'd eat.

When the sun started to sink from view and there were no fishermen left on the beach, Tony would take off my clothes and kiss me all over. He didn't take his off. Sometimes he did. I closed my eyes and let him do everything to me: I imagined he was Gustavo and that we were in Venice. Tony was perfect, but he couldn't take me to Venice. Sometimes, he took me to the cinema. One day we saw a romantic film that ended with a death, her death. And Tony cried and held me very tight: don't die.

What I liked most about having sex on the beach was the sky. Tony's face would appear and disappear from my line of sight, alternating with the sky blue background. Up and down, up and down. I didn't move; I just lay there, looking at the clouds. I put my hands behind the back of my neck, as if I was doing sit-ups, and waited for Tony to finish. Then he'd lie down next to me, all hot and bothered, and I'd talk to him:

The first time I saw a sailboat was in the harbour. My father took me there, I was two and a half.

But that was a lie. Another day, I told him something different:

The first time I saw a sailboat was inside a bottle. My father bought it for me at the craft fair and told me: when you grow up, we'll go sailing in one like that. And I said to him: As small as that?

But this was a lie too.

Once, Tony told me I was frigid, but then he regretted it. He knelt down in front of me, kissed my hands and kept saying sorry, sorry, sorry. What happens is that I get distracted looking at the gannets, I told him, because it seemed a bit lame to say the thing about the sky. Then he had the idea of doing it the other way around. He lay back on the towel and I climbed on top of him, so now I could only look at his face. Tony didn't like looking at the sky. He liked grabbing my hair as if it were vines, and looking into my eyes, absorbed. I became addicted to this position. I became addicted to Tony.

My routine went like this: go to the gym with Tony, go out on Tony's bike, have sex with Tony either, 1) on the beach, 2) in a cheap motel room, or 3) on the deserted terrace of a city centre hotel, where we'd walk in wearing dark glasses, like tourists seeking a glimpse of a panoramic view. On the terrace we would do it at midday, when the sun had already scared everyone away; we would do it standing up, me in front, against the balcony railing, with Tony taking me from behind. We would leave again swiftly, jump back on the bike and head to a kiosk to buy Coca-Cola and cigarettes. We talked about old movies, salsa songs and things we wanted to buy ourselves. Tony liked Calvin Klein fragrances, but he'd never had one: his mother never quite had enough money to buy one for him. Now he worked at his uncle's stationery shop, but he still didn't have enough.

Are you happy? he would ask, towards the end of the evening, as we lay beneath a tree in a park. I told him I was, because it was true. But something was missing. I knew what it was; Tony didn't.

My father was far from pleased about me leaving university, and he told me as much, every time we crossed paths. I'd be arriving home, and he'd be setting out, at six, seven in the morning. I explained to him: I want to leave, and a degree in law is only useful in the country where you study it. Study something else. What? Anything, but study something, you're the bright one, you're our great hope. And he'd wink at me. Hope of what? My brother told me I should become an air hostess, that they'd give me the visa automatically and I would have more chances of getting out of here, at least for periods at a time. We were in his bedroom, it smelled of the Mexsana talcum powder he used to put on his feet. He was lifting dumbbells in front of the mirror and counting backwards: 33, 32, 31, 30… Why do you count backwards? I asked him. He told me it was more motivating that way: because One did not move, did not get further away, it was there, where it had always been, at the beginning. I thought that my brother was the smart one, but I didn't tell him.

The next day, after the gym, I went to sign up for an air hostess course. If I liked it, I could carry on and get the diploma. Tony didn't like the idea, because air hostesses aren't shown any respect, he said. They are basically just trolley dollies, with men ogling their asses as they walk down those narrow aisles. If a guy grabs an air hostess's ass, she just has to smile. And if they don't let men grab their asses, it's worse, because then they're badly treated. If the toilet is out of order, they have to go and unblock it with a drinking straw. If the food is off, they have to eat it anyway, to keep up appearances. Tony had a lot of ideas about air hostesses, but I had just one: air hostesses could leave.

6

Brígida must have been pretty old, but she didn't look it.

Black women don't age, my mother used to say.

Brígida had dense hair in her armpits, stuck together with white clumps because of the bicarb she applied to stop herself smelling. She smelled anyway. A cruise ship had come in and Brígida stopped by Gustavo's shack for some oysters. It was Thursday. I didn't have to go to the Institute on Thursdays, and since I wasn't going out with Tony anymore, sometimes I went to visit Gustavo. I lounged in the hammock reading magazines in English, for practice.

That Thursday, Brígida asked me the same thing she always asked me: whether I had a husband yet. No. If I had a boyfriend yet. I don't know. And she laughed.

Lately, Brígida was going around with a granddaughter in tow, who frowned at me, her lips pursed. I ignored her, flipping the pages of my magazine, yawning now and again. Lately, it was Olga who saw to Brígida: she dealt with the oysters, negotiated the price, gulped one down and then talked to her about the product as if she was an expert on the matter. Brígida didn't like oysters, only once did I see her swallow one. She screwed up her face – you could really see her age then – and then she spat it out and said: that's like chewing on a pussy.

While Olga dealt with Brígida and I read in English and the granddaughter silently cursed me, Gustavo, at the worktable, told a story. The story would start with a

21

precise anecdote and would end up god-knows-where. For example:

When I lived in Valparaíso, father had various market stalls and he had me peeling prawns until my fingers were swollen. He taught me how to peel a prawn: you grab it firmly by the tail, carefully pull off the head so that that it doesn't bring all the meat with it, and then you take off the legs. The shell comes off on its own. And you leave the tail.

What do you leave it for? I interrupted sometimes, because if not, it would be like he was talking to himself, and I felt sorry for him.

So that the shape of the animal stays intact, it's more elegant like that.

I don't see anything elegant about it.

All the flavour's in the tail, that's why you have to suck it.

Suck it? Gross.

The tail holds the elixir of the animal, the soul of the animal, the essence of the animal.

Right.

It's all there: in the tail.

Mm-hm.

After a while, Olga also tried to get involved, but she would say things that were completely irrelevant. Things like: the day before yesterday I saw a group of *gringos* walking through the city centre, their legs were covered in pus-filled blisters. And, as nobody replied, she would get bored and grumble her way into the shack and switch on the little TV that her sister had sent over from Venezuela.

And her in there and us out here.

I opened a beer, fanned myself with the magazine. Later I opened another beer, and one for Gustavo. The sun would get really strong, and it was hard to find a position in the hammock where I wouldn't be blinded it by it. Gustavo went on:

…I remember that about Valparaíso, and I also remember Silvina. Silvina had thick, shiny hair that she wore in a high ponytail, and a colourful dress that she wore at weekends.

Just one?

I liked that dress because every time she wore it, she would bend down to me and ask, Do I look pretty, *guagüita?*

Gua-what?

Silvina was the last girlfriend of father's that I met, because after that summer I never saw him again. He took a job on a ship and never came back. I went to Argentina.

Why Argentina?

Because that's where mother was.

Hadn't she been thrown into the sea?

…and once, father sent a letter, saying he was in Brazil, and that he had a girlfriend, not Silvina, but Mary-Erin, who was young and pretty.

And where was Niní?

…in the letter, father told me to get on a bus and go see him, that mother could pay for my journey and he would pay her back from there.

Why do you always say mother and father?

How else should I refer to them?

My mother, and *my* father, like everyone else does. Otherwise you sound like a character in a badly dubbed movie: like when you say *luncheon*, or *valise* or *stockings*, or *motorcar*, or *galoshes*.

I don't say any of those things.

Yes, you do.

7

My first flight was to Miami. It was the city's busiest international route, and the most sought-after. I went for it, and I got it. I wanted to go to Miami because it was cheap to buy things there, the weather was good, and the men weren't *gringos*. The young air hostesses didn't like *gringos* because they were bad in bed; the old ones did, because they took whatever they could get.

Do you know Miami? I asked Julián. He said he did, but I could tell he was lying. Julián was watching TV in our living room: there was a boxing match on. My brother was in the shower, getting ready to go to a party. My mother, on the phone to my grandmother: the cousin of a relative had died. My father had gone out to pay some traffic fines.

Do you know Miami? I asked Gustavo. He didn't reply. Olga snorted. He was drinking rum in the hammock, looking out to sea. Olga was grating coconut for a rice dish. She had a long white skirt and red knickers on, her tits spilling out of a tight, low-cut black Lycra top.

I had gone to say goodbye.

In Miami, I stayed in a hotel near the airport. I had already arranged for a friend of a friend from the gym to come and meet me. He was married but he turned up without his wife. Probably for the best, seeing as lately I had not been getting on with anybody's wives: young air hostesses were notorious for spreading their legs in any airport toilet. Old air hostesses were notorious for spitting in the plane food, among other things. My colleague Susana said that the old air hostesses suffered from terrible flatulence – a result of so many years eating that shrink-wrapped food – which became uncontrollable at certain altitudes.

This friend of a friend was called Juan, but he was known as Johnny, and he was a huge, green-eyed, mixed race guy. His car still had that "new car" smell. He took me out to eat some spicy food and then he took me for a ride along Ocean Drive. Before going back to the hotel, we went into a bar owned by Johnny's friend – an associate, he said, then corrected himself: a buddy, and slapped him on the back. We drank Negronis. I'd never had a Negroni, but I didn't say so. Do you like it? asked Johnny, and I nodded: I like strong drinks. He clinked his glass with mine and breathed into my ear, *me like you, beibi.*

Johnny smelled of expensive cologne.

I had to get back to the hotel by midnight because the Captain said he didn't want any of us staying out all night. Our flight was at seven. Thanks, Johnny, I had a great time. He lunged in for a kiss, but I dodged it. Johnny wasn't bad looking, but if he got his way now, I wouldn't have anyone to call next time I came to Miami. I was planning to go to Miami often, until I found a way to stay there for good.

When I got back, the rain started. Again, like it had not rained for years. Days and days of torrential rain, which meant we were unable to fly: the airport was closed, and I was bored, watching films about people who were happy for the first half an hour and who then got sad, and that's what it was all about, getting over the sadness. Then something would happen, and they ended up even happier than they were at the start.

I had moved out of my parent's house months ago and was living with Milagros, a girl who sold alcohol in the duty-free shop and had put up a notice in the toilets:

looking for a roommate, two-bed apartment near the airport. I liked the idea of living near the airport, so I could be 100% available for the airline. If someone was ill, I was there in five minutes to replace them. If a charter flight was leaving and they needed staff, I would volunteer myself. Every time a plane took off or landed, I knew about it.

I liked the sound of the aeroplanes.

On the third day of rain, I put on a raincoat and went to visit Gustavo, but it was Olga's head that poked out of the door to the shack. Where's Gustavo? And she said: he's gone fishing. The sky was falling in sheets of water. I didn't move. Olga emerged to stand in the doorway, revealing her naked body, dark and glossy, her magic button a tangled mat of hair.

I left.

I called my parents' house, it felt like years since I'd heard from them. As soon as my mother started talking, I realised that everything was the same: she had fallen out with one of my aunts, because my aunt was a manipulator who liked to bleed my grandmother dry. Me: bleed her dry of what? Her: what do you think? My father had hired a new driver, because the last one had stolen from him. He'd taken three hundred thousand pesos and the spare tyre. Did you report it? No, what would be the point? It never does any good. Right. What about my brother? Out and about.

The block of flats where I lived with Milagros was near the sea. When it rained, an eerie-sounding wind blew. Tony called me occasionally. I told him I didn't want to see him. On one of those rainy nights, it was me who called him.

Do you want to go and see a film? I don't know, I don't think so. Are you with someone? No. You're with someone.

Tony lived far from me, it would have taken almost an hour on the bus, but he took a taxi and arrived in twenty minutes. I was in the shower. He must have spent all his money for the week. Tony turned on a film on the TV in the living room, and Milagros shut herself away in her bedroom. See you tomorrow, she said. I came out in pyjamas, smelling of soap. Before I sat down, I went to the kitchen to get the Guatemalan rum that Milagros had brought home. I took a swig from the bottle and then poured a glass for Tony, who barely wet his lips with it. I sat down and immediately climbed on top of him. I had no idea what film he'd put on. The first time, I came. The second, he did. When we had finished, Tony said: marry me.

I can't. Why? Because of work. What's that got to do with it? I'd leave you on your own all the time, and I'd get so jealous imagining that when I'm not there, you'd replace me with someone else. You're irreplaceable. I am now, but when I leave you alone, you'll realise I'm not. Let's go to Canada. Canada is full of old people. Quit your job. Never. But why not? Never in a million years.

He left.

It was still raining. Out of the window, the lights in the street looked distorted. Across the street, there was a huge illuminated sign for a fried chicken restaurant, but that night it was a shapeless blur. I went over to the window, wiped it and looked down. Tony was there, standing on the corner, looking around the street, waiting for something to happen. Nothing happened.

I thought about opening the window and shouting to him to come back up. I thought about opening the window and shouting, Yes! But what I actually did was light a cigarette, and still watching him, I imagined my life with him. It went like this:

It is raining. I leave the airport, heading for a tiny apartment in a neighbourhood miles away, overlooking a rotten swamp. I have plastic bags in my handbag to put on my feet when I get off the bus, so my heels don't get stuck in the mud when I'm walking home. On the way to the building, I have to dodge kids screaming and splashing around on the pavements. I am deafened by the *vallenato* music booming out of the low, cramped houses, from which a sickly-yellow light seeps. It smells of fried food, it smells of rum, it smells of rotten swamp, it smells of poverty. Hi, sweetheart, Tony says, opening the door. In his arms is a small child, slurping at its own snot. Soon, that baby will be slurping at my tits. Then we eat a watery lentil stew, we go to bed and turn off the light. Tony would cling to my back like a limpet, his arm around my waist, and whisper in my ear: one day we'll get out of here. Me: we'll always be here, waiting for a hurricane to come.

By the time I finished my cigarette, Tony was still there, but I wasn't.

8

Johnny knew a guy. As simple as that. That's how Johnny was, you'd say to him: I'd love to multiply my savings by a thousand. Him: I know a guy. I'd love to travel to Cuba, to buy some cigars and come back. What for? To sell them. I know a guy. I'd love to get a tattoo. Where? On the back of my neck. I know a guy. I'd love to stay here forever. And that's when Johnny didn't know anyone. He said: this is a very hard country. But he lived like a tycoon, he got a new car every six months and went on paying the same lease. He received unemployment benefit that nobody checked up on, and that was what paid for the motels where we fucked, or the lobster we ate at Key West, or the VIP passes for the salsa bars he took me to in Little Havana. Johnny lived off money from his wife – half *gringa*, half Ecuadorian – and he even bought designer underpants. He zealously fed his little American dream in fear that if he forgot to feed it one day, it would keel over in front of him like a starving baby bird.

Maybe I should stop seeing you and find a *gringo* to marry, I'd say to him. And Johnny would lunge at me, push me against the wall and shove his hand up my skirt: come here, *beibi*. Because Johnny was a whore, he wanted to resolve everything in the bedroom. Let go of me, you bastard. I'd push him off me and leave.

I was always in a bad mood on the way back and the Captain began to notice. Did you quarrel with your boyfriend? The Captain always spoke to me very formally.

No, sir, I don't have a boyfriend. What a waste. On that flight there were four air hostesses, two old ones and Susana and me. Susana insisted that the Captain was in love with me. I knew which part of me the Captain was in love with: he could barely tear his eyes off my ass. But he had nothing to offer me in return.

Then, my brother struck gold. He wrote me an email telling me he was getting married: her name was Odina and she was Puerto Rican, but she lived in Los Angeles. He had met her online; as he didn't have a visa, she had come to see him, and Bob's your uncle, they sealed their love. He didn't introduce me to her because I was flying, or so my mother had told him. He described her as beautiful, brown-skinned and slim, and she came with the right dowry: the green card. I called the airline, told them I was really ill and then shut myself away for three days to cry: 88, 87, 86... And that's how I fell asleep, obsessing over my brother. I was sure the whole thing about pushing me to become an air hostess had been his strategy to get me away from the only computer in the house, where he chatted all day long, year after year, looking for a wife, until he stumbled upon that Puerto Rican bitch.

They had a church wedding here, and a civil ceremony there. My brother, in his correspondence with her, had made out that he was incredibly religious. On Odina's side, there was a large party of friends and relatives. Common as muck, the lot of them. On our side, we had some second cousins from a village. Also common as muck. They all had children, and they all dressed the same. In the church, a girl sat next to me and told me that when she grew up she was going to come to the city and work for a company. Her hair was combed in segments, hard and crispy with hair spray. I imagined her in the city, a few years older, working from sun-up to sun-down in a little stuffy office that she would travel to and from on the minibus. She would bring her lunch in a Tupperware box, and dye her hair with cheap blond dye that would turn orange in the sun, so she'd switch to a copper mahogany tone.

The priest gave a sermon about good love, intended for procreation, and bad love, intended for enjoyment. Then an emaciated nun sang the Ave Maria.

The celebration took place in a large, ramshackle old house in the city centre. Odina's family paid for it, because in line with tradition, the bride paid for the party and the groom paid for the honeymoon. There would not be a honeymoon right away because Odina had to go back to work. Odina was a nurse. Odina was far from "slim". She was fat. Odina's parents were classic "wannabe" types. So were mine, though they didn't even know what it meant to be "wannabes". That night, there were so many white fairy lights strung up around the terrace it was like being part of some Caribbean royalty. The L-shaped buffet table was overflowing with hundreds of hot and cold dishes: mainly seafood. Gustavo was the supplier, although my father hadn't bought fish from him for years because his prices had gone up so much. They had invited Gustavo to the party, but he excused himself. I don't go to parties, he said. Nobody insisted. It would have been awkward to explain the presence of that hairy old man, stinking of fish and all leathery from the sun, tucked away in a corner with his bottle of rum. And his black girlfriend.

Didn't you invite Olga? I asked my mother. Olga who? she said. Gustavo's girlfriend. My mother had no idea who I was talking about.

In the toilets they had all kinds of perfumes to overpower the smell of dancefloor sweat. On the tables were Polaroid cameras for the guests to use. On the dance floor there were tiny holes that pumped out a floral-scented mist. At midnight they let off fireworks spelling out the names of the bride and groom in the sky; followed by more which read *Just Married,* in English. A trio sang boleros, then an orchestra played and later, after the dinner, a DJ took over, flooding the elegant perfumed air of the celebration with reggaeton, which "Odi" was crazy about. Odi's hips swayed like a poisonous snake, and yet my mother and father gazed at her like she was some kind of angelic apparition. Every so often they would let out a sigh and look at each other and nod, no doubt thinking: we've struck gold. Odina called them mummy this, daddy that, and she called me "sistah". She threw the bouquet straight into my arms, but I stepped back out of the way, letting it fall to the floor. There followed a couple of bewildered seconds when everyone expected me to bend down and pick it up, but instead I turned and walked towards the door.

Tony was just arriving: he'd said he wasn't coming because he had to work late at the stationery shop. His uncle had made him a partner, big fucking deal. Like all the men, he was wearing white trousers and a coloured shirt – turquoise, in his case. He had gelled his hair and combed it back, like mobsters do. He had a goatee, and although he said hello and kissed me on the cheek, he gave me a resentful look. I asked him why he was arriving so late and he said: I just finished work and thought, why not go and congratulate my buddy? Apparently, they were buddies now, but when Tony was going out with me, my brother thought he was a failure, a *fokin' loozer*, a small-town waste of space, a broke guy who'd never give me what I deserved. What did I deserve? My brother reeled off some things – things I couldn't remember now – while I traced lines between them, sewing them together, drawing a tangled web.

Aren't you coming in? Tony was still standing at the door, looking at me. From inside, my brother's deep, husky voice drifted out, singing *I want to tell you everything I like about you…* You missed the photo for the newspaper, I said to him. He didn't reply, just clenched his teeth.

Julián had dated the girl in charge of the social section of the paper; apparently, she had promised him a half-page spread. This was no mean feat, as there were queues of people waiting to get their faces in there.

On the night of the wedding, this was the photo:

In the centre, the bride and groom in pure white apart from Odi's bright red lips. Then the women, two mothers and a grandmother, ancient divas in their organza dresses printed with wild flowers. The two fathers, in garish shirts: one parrot green, one bright orange. The best man, Julián, accompanied as always by his obscene biceps, this time with some scrawny eye-candy hanging off them, dressed in yellow. The bridesmaids: on one side was Odi's friend Tanya, a smoking hot Cuban in a sparkly top with a plunging neckline, very "bling", and on the other side was me, dressed all in black like I was at a funeral, champagne in hand, looking anywhere but at the lens.

The day the newspaper came out, there was the photo, but in black and white. It seemed Julián didn't have enough sway to get a page in colour.

Let's go in, insisted Tony. I turned my back on him and lit a cigarette.

The sound of his new shoes going into the party, moving away from me yet again, made my belly ache with sadness. But not for me, or for him; but for the fishermen's beach where we used to screw, which was now a hotel. And for the terrace of the hotel where we used to screw, which was no longer there. For the wasted years.

After that night I never saw him again. Or at least, not until much later.

9

Johnny knew a guy who brought merchandise down from the United States. You ordered the product on Amazon, giving the address of the guy there, and he came down with his suitcases like a tourist and didn't declare anything. He charged by the weight of the package, not the volume, and according to Johnny that was a major advantage, one which I couldn't care less about. He was known as Santa Claus because the guy mostly carried toys for children for Christmas; they were much cheaper up there. And now, this guy that Johnny knew had a new business and that was what he wanted to talk to me about. The guy rents himself out as a relative of pregnant women, Johnny said. I don't understand the business, I said. We were in a snack bar in Kendall, eating hot wings. My fingers were slathered in red sauce, and I had to lick them to stop it dripping everywhere.

Johnny ordered two more beers. The snack bar was almost empty: just the owner, a nice guy from the Dominican Republic, his daughter, who was wearing a polka dot miniskirt that was far too short on her, considering her age and shape; and a young couple in the corner with their tongues down each other's throats. When the daughter brought over the beers, Johnny – after a long look at the miniskirt – explained the guy's business to me. He brings women over here to give birth, he pretends he's an uncle or a cousin of theirs, and he looks after them in his house for the last three months of the pregnancy, because after that they aren't allowed to travel. He gets a doctor friend to see them during that time and then he takes them to the hospital to give birth. And then he vanishes, so they can't link him to it. So, what's the point? I asked him. What do you think? said Johnny, the kid is born a *gringo*, and then they automatically give you nationality. He winked at me, which reminded me of my father. You bastard, I said to him. Him: don't say that Johnny doesn't love you. I sat on his lap and kissed him eagerly: Johnny loves me, I said into his ear. The girl in the miniskirt was watching us out of the corner of her eye, twirling a lock of hair around her forefinger. I asked Johnny for the guy's number.

When I got back, I found Gustavo alone, peeling prawns at his worktable. There was a strong breeze, the tarpaulin roof was flapping around. Where's Olga? At the market. Right. I stretched out in the hammock and after a while it occurred to me to ask about the children. What children? Don't you have children? He remained lost in thought for a minute, then said:

In Bolivia, I lived in a house with thirteen people. The landlady was a woman called Rosita.

And you had a child with Rosita?

No. In that house, every night somebody would cook dinner, we all ate together and sang songs, and some of them got naked and fucked on the floor. But I didn't. And neither did Rosita. Rosita took off her blouse and made me touch her breasts and tell her what I felt. I felt scared, but I never told her that.

What did you tell her?

I told her: your breasts are like white seashells.

Right.

The guy that Johnny knew was called Ever and he was a real ugly so-and-so. He weighed about two hundred kilos and his face was mottled with patches of vitiligo. He charged a shitload of money, but he was a sure thing, he said, not like those guys who promise you a green card and you wind up with a Blockbuster membership. How much do you have left? What, money? No, I mean of the pregnancy. I lied: not much. He told me to think about it and to tell Johnny if I wanted to go ahead. The guy spoke in a whisper because it was a delicate subject, he said. I had to lean closer to him over the table and inhale his breath. It smelled like someone who had just eaten a mountain of sardines. When he finally finished talking, he heaved his enormous body up and dragged it to the door of the Denny's; he reached his arms up in a lazy stretch, and tyres of fat rippled over the top of his waistband. I thought I wouldn't be able to stand one day in that guy's care. Anyway. The plan was a non-starter for me. Not the getting pregnant part – a kid could be made in any airport toilet, but because of the money. As always, the money.

Why so pensive? the Captain said to me. We were in the airline lounge, waiting for them to finish cleaning the plane. No reason, I replied. Susana was not on the flight that day, the others were there, and Flor: ugly, bitter, haggard Flor. She even walked funny; nobody could get their heads round how she'd become an air hostess. The Captain said, would you like to have a drink with me one day? He looked into my eyes, but only because I was sitting down. Flor cleared her throat and left the tiny room, her steps like a crippled heron. Out of the window, a plane was landing, the sky glowed with blue and violet hues. I don't know, I said to the Captain, holding his gaze. Maybe.

10

It was Odina who got pregnant and gave birth and, as my parents didn't have a visa to go to the US, my brother, the Puerto Potty and their kid came down as soon as possible so they could meet their grandchild. Odina had put on about a hundred kilos and still insisted on calling me "sistah". The child looked just like her; they named him Simón. They slept in my brother's old bedroom and the baby slept in mine. The walls had been painted blue and on the bedside table there was a basket filled with little blue organza bags containing blue sweets, with "Baby boy" written on the wrapper. A souvenir of your visit to see the baby. I saw them the first day and then I disappeared. I told them I had two flights back to back, and a long stopover in Seattle. Nobody seemed to be listening.

I had never been to Seattle. I had never flown anywhere in the United States other than Miami. But I knew the country off by heart, thanks to the Pato Banton song *Go Pato*. Sometimes I used to recite the names of the states while I was in the shower. When I got to the apartment I called the airline and asked if they needed any reserve staff. We're full, they told me. I shut myself away in my bedroom: 54, 53, 52, 51… There were cracks in the ceiling. Milagros had a French boyfriend. The Captain had been calling me a lot lately, we had gone out once, without much success. The Captain was from one of the provinces, and I didn't like people from there because they spoke slowly and way too formally. But those were hard times, so I called him: we arranged to meet at a little Italian place, in the city centre.

The Latin American style is one of cliché, he said to me halfway through dinner, after I'd told him the story of my brother, the wedding with cameras on the tables, the white fairy lights and perfumes in the toilet and the "Baby boy". I thought it was quite a clever observation and I thought that my future child wouldn't have it too bad, with 1) a decent set of neurons, and 2) a tolerance for heights. That night we stayed at his, an apartment in El Laguito, with a panoramic window overlooking the bay. It was very beautiful, but it was still *here*.

The Captain was genuinely in awe of my ass; it's more beautiful than I imagined, he said.

But I didn't get pregnant. Not that time, or any of the following times. I went to the gynaecologist to ask if there was something wrong with me. I was fine, it had to be him. It was going to be hard to ask him, the man thought I was on the pill.

Have you got any children? I asked him one evening, smoking a cigarette, looking out at the bay. The lighthouse had already come on, the rotating beam passed over us like brushstrokes on a mural. I enjoyed that moment. I hoped he wouldn't answer, but it was too late. The Captain didn't have children. Would you like to, one day…? Halfway through the question I already regretted it. Years ago, said the Captain, I had a vasectomy for medical reasons. Medical reasons! I felt betrayed, taken for a fool. The Captain looked at me, baffled. I put my clothes on and left.

I walked along the boardwalk, first around the edge of the bay, then the sea, then the sea walls, then a heap of rubble on a deserted beach. There, I sat down and cried. The evening was red, it was the most beautiful sky I had seen in years. From the Captain's window it must have been just spectacular. I found a payphone and called him. He didn't answer. I tried again, nothing. I hailed a taxi and went home.

The beak of the illuminated sign for the fried chicken place had burnt out and was dark.

And it started raining again: in a town near the Magdalena river even the dogs drowned. In a hamlet close to the Ciénaga de la Virgen, four children and a teacher died. They were trapped inside a Social Welfare centre that got swept away by the current. On the radio, they were talking about the Submarine Outfall again: a Dutch company was going to start building it. The national government tendered the work out to foreign companies because the national ones had already stolen the money three times. But the Dutch didn't steal.

Johnny sent me an email: I miss you, baby. And another one, in English this time: *I miss u, beibi.*

I thought of going to see Gustavo. The last time had been about six months earlier, a bright, sunny day, and it went like this:

I sat down at the worktable and the smell of fish made me feel sick. I suggested we go for a walk to get a change of air. As we walked, he told me that Olga had gone: her sister had come to get her from Venezuela. I couldn't believe that anyone would choose to go to Venezuela. Even a slut like Olga could surely aspire to something better than going to Venezuela. She'd be better off here. We walked along the beach for hours, and finally sat down in a canoe that was falling to pieces and filled with crabs. I was thirsty. I asked about Willy. He died, said Gustavo. Of what? He shrugged. And Brígida? She died. Liar. I don't know about Brígida, he said after a while. What about Willy? Or him.

This time I had brought him an umbrella and a small arsenal of vices: cigarettes, beer, rum, some weed. He rolled a cigarette and poured a couple of rums. He was wearing long trousers; I couldn't remember ever seeing him in long trousers. He was going bald. He was getting old. The rain stops me from working, he complained, gesturing at the churning waves. Me too, I said, looking up at the clouds. Gustavo's pool was filled with stagnant water; there were dead fish floating on the surface. The larger creatures must have been lurking somewhere in the depths. The tarpaulin was ripped in various places and water was streaming through it. The driest place was the double wooden seat, although it was also damp. Water and wood are not good friends, I said to Gustavo. We sat down.

Tell me a story.

I've already told you all of them.

Tell me a story with me in it.

Gustavo sighed heavily and shook his head. It's a sad story.

I don't mind.

I curled up next to him. I laid my head on his scrawny, smelly lap. He began stroking my hair.

Once upon a time, there was a sweet, noble princess who had only one flaw: she couldn't tell the difference between what was good and bad, beautiful and hideous, diabolical and heavenly, perverse and pure...

I fell asleep.

11

The next flight to Miami was hell. And the ones after that. The Captain was avoiding me and now seemed more interested in Susana who, as she had no ass to speak of, had started sporting a very revealing push-up bra. I couldn't care less because I had my Johnny, who was becoming more attentive and affectionate; he'd given me a laptop, so we could chat. I told him about the city: that in the centre they were building mansions that were filling up with celebrities. Julio Iglesias, Caroline of Monaco, Mick Jagger, Lady Gaga – they all had houses there. Johnny didn't seem very impressed. All Johnny wanted was for me to turn on the webcam and talk dirty to him while I touched myself. And I did, but not always. I thought: one day Johnny will come to his senses, he'll know what to do.

Johnny was becoming flaky.

The last time I saw him, he took me to the same dive bar with the buffalo wings, in Kendall. He was distracted, sullen, eyeing up the Dominican slut, who appeared to have developed huge matronly hips overnight. At some point, a well-dressed woman stood at the doorway and surveyed the place. Johnny said, she doesn't think it looks clean enough for her to sit her bony ass down. He sounded bitter, resentful. Then he fell silent again. What's up? I asked him. He said there was nothing wrong. We went to a motel, we fucked, he lit a cigarette and went silent again. I switched on the TV, nothing happened, it was broken.

On the flight back, Susana avoided me. I said to her: Johnny's going to ask me to marry him and she said, Great! But it sounded false.

Then one day, Johnny stood me up. I was waiting in the lobby of the hotel. I was all dressed up to go salsa dancing: hair in a ponytail, shiny trousers, jangly metal bracelet. Suddenly I felt ridiculous. I called his home phone number, his wife answered, and before I'd finished asking for him, she was shouting at me, *holly shit, you fokin puta!* Then she threatened to shoot me three times in the pussy. There was a pause, during which I suppose she was catching her breath to start insulting me again, and I seized the opportunity to say: look, lady, Johnny knocked me up. And I hung up.

Going back was miserable. When I got to the apartment, I collapsed on the living room sofa, staring out the window: the chicken sign wasn't lit up. It wouldn't be until later. I didn't eat, I didn't go to the toilet, all I did was think about Johnny and stare at the grimy window pane. 19, 18, 17, 16…

Johnny didn't appear online. I sent him three hundred and seventeen emails. Nothing. I never heard from him again. And with time, the sadness passed, but I was filled with pity. Firstly, for him, because he must have lost everything: his car, his unemployment benefit, his Ecuadorian wife, his VIP passes, his dignity. Then for me, because I'd lost my drives around Miami, the lobster and champagne, the sunsets in Mallory Square, the good life that Johnny had got me used to. And then for me, again for me, for the many times in my life, for every time I'd lost someone I didn't even care about.

12

I took some time off once and didn't know where to go. They made me take time off because, according to my boss, I had never taken any holiday and I had to. Why? Because it's a new policy. I thought that there was something wrong with this new policy, and I told her as much, but she took no notice. It was a very small airline and they were tendering to move up a category, to get more routes. During those days off I visited my mother and the first thing she did was show me photos of a boy aged three, four years old, dressed as a cowboy, dressed as Snoopy, dressed as Tarzan. Who's that? I asked. Who? That child. She shot me a furious look: Simón, your nephew! I didn't know what to say. While my mother grumbled away, I realised that she had become an old woman: she had grey hairs and wrinkles, and the stale breath that comes with age.

I stayed for dinner.

My father had finally given up the taxi business for good, but he was still complaining: nobody takes cares of things that aren't theirs. A letter came for you, said my mother. When? She squinted and said: it was over a year ago. Why didn't you let me know? I don't have your phone number. Yes, you do. She waved me away with her hand: pah!

I got back to the apartment at midnight. I opened the windows; it was hot. A breeze wafted in, smelling of sludge.

The letter was from Maritza Caballero, my teenage friend. She said she hadn't heard from me in a long time, and as she only had that address for me, she had taken a chance on writing to me there, although she presumed I had probably moved. For a while we used to write letters to one another, but then I stopped replying. I got bored. According to what she told me, Medellín was a shitty city. It was neither cold nor hot, pretty nor ugly, rich nor poor. Medellín was nothing. Anyway, she didn't live in Medellín anymore, but in Panama. Her father had been posted to Peru many years ago. She had gone back and forth many times, and now she had settled in Panama with her husband, who worked on the Canal, and her children. She enclosed a photo of her; she looked the same but with crow's feet and a guy next to her, a girl and a boy sitting at their feet, like pets. Her phone number, in case I ever went to Panama, was... I scrunched the letter up into a ball and hurled it at the fried chicken, right at the beak, but it didn't quite make it. It landed in the middle of the street.

I lit a cigarette.

I didn't go to Gustavo's because I didn't feel like it. I didn't go anywhere. I called the Captain, he didn't pick up. I called again. A woman answered. Hello? Susana? Who is this? I hung up. But it wasn't Susana, she had a funny accent.

On Friday, Milagros invited me to go to the islands with them. Her French boyfriend and some friends had rented a couple of cabins. I shaved my legs, packed a bag and then waited with Milagros for them to pick us up. A car with a driver came to collect us and dropped us off down at the quay. Then a boat came in, full of foreigners and hookers. I looked at Milagros, who shrugged. What were you expecting? I thought for two or three seconds. I realised I wasn't expecting anything. We went aboard. A Frenchman sat down next to me and asked me if I had my life jacket on properly. I said *Oui*. When we arrived at the beach there was a buffet of juices and drinks. What are you drinking? asked the Frenchman. Negroni. He looked at the table: I don't think they have it. Cuba Libre, I said. He nodded and went to get some ice.

We were in a hut filled with wicker sofas. Some of the men had gone off to the beach with their hookers; Milagros and her boyfriend were smooching in one of the cabins. There were two Frenchmen left, who were touching up a girl who couldn't even have been eighteen. She was laughing. She seemed nervous, but she was hiding it well.

My Frenchman returned with the drinks. We sat down on a sofa and he put his arm around my shoulder. It was limp, cold, toad-like. I shrugged his arm off and said: I'm expensive. Very expensive? Yes. I don't care. Okay: I held out my hand, palm up.

We came back on the Monday, badly hungover. I still had a week of holiday left and I didn't know what else to do. Spend the money from the Frenchman, but on what, where? I would have been totally justified in spending it on a rent boy who could actually give me a good seeing-to. I called the Captain, but the same woman answered. I hung up. It wasn't like the Captain was even that good in bed. Then I called Tony's house. His mother told me that he'd moved years ago, and when I insisted, she gave me his mobile number. Hello? He answered. I miss you, I told him. He was silent for a minute and then said: I don't. I bought you a present. What? You're going to like it. I don't want it. Are you sure? What is it? A surprise: if you come I'll give it to you, if not… you'll never know. I don't know… Come. I got married. I don't care. I do. I'll see you in an hour.

I had bought him a Calvin Klein fragrance. He stayed for the rest of the week.

13

Simón fell ill and, as my parents did not have a visa to go to the US, they asked me to go and see him. They begged me: they came to my apartment for the first time ever and they begged. I told them: I've already taken all my holiday. Them: it's a family emergency, we've never asked you for anything, he's our only grandchild. My boss pursed her lips: didn't you use all your holiday? It's a family emergency, I've never asked you for anything, he's my only nephew. She granted me ten days of unpaid leave.

My mother had become obsessed with the idea that God was punishing her for what happened with Xenaida's child, and she got some concoction made up by a "specialist" who my aunt knew. She gave it to me in a bottle, so I could rub it on the little boy's chest. It smelled like dead rats. It made me want to vomit, so I poured it down the toilet and threw the bottle in the bin. I washed my hands thoroughly and covered them in the Victoria's Secret antibacterial gel we'd been given by the airline for Christmas.

Before I left, I dropped in at Gustavo's shack. It was not raining, but he was not fishing. He hadn't fished for days because one of his legs hurt and his bones ached, he said. I told him I was off to Los Angeles and that maybe I was going to stay there. That if my brother hinted at it, I would stay. Why not? Maybe I would meet someone. Someone who would give me what I deserved. Gustavo asked what it was that I deserved. I stared at him: his white hair had become wiry; his skin, a paper-thin cloth draped over his bones. How old was Gustavo? A thousand? I had never asked him his age. I shrugged. He poured two small glasses of rum. The bottle was nearly empty. He handed me one, raised his glass up in front of him, to the sea:

We'll always have this view, kid.

I knocked back the rum in one go: Goodbye.

In Los Angeles it was raining too, and this was unusual. A miracle, according to Odina. Hadn't I seen *Chinatown*, she asked. No. Well it's just like that, she said, dry as limestone.

It sure hid it well.

It rained a lot, but nobody there drowned: least of all the dogs, who were dressed up like children in little hooded raincoats. Odina worked long shifts at the hospital, and when she came home, she complained about her feet being swollen. Then she would look in the mirror: I'm a *fokin whale*! she shouted, angry, nobody knew who with. I looked elsewhere, as if I hadn't heard her. My brother had a job driving a delivery truck. Delivering what? Fruit, vegetables, local farm produce. *Eat local, stay local,* it said on his grey shirt. How's Julián? I asked him one night. He was flicking through the channels. Odina was on a shift; Simón was asleep. He didn't know what Julián was up to. And Rafa? Rafa who? That friend of yours who… But he was glued to the screen, a baseball game was on. His perfect abs were buried under a big belly. It must've been because of all the beer he drank. It must've been because of marriage. I wonder what happened to Xenaida's child? I said after a while. My brother didn't reply, perhaps he hadn't heard me, or perhaps he just didn't give a shit.

Simón was looked after by a very young girl who spent the whole time chewing gum and listening to music on oversized wireless headphones. The house was made from wood, like the ones in the movies. It was comfortable, but it was no mansion. Sure, there were household appliances everywhere you looked, and the fridge was overflowing with food. All the food looked succulent and appetising, but it tasted of absolutely nothing. Macaroni and cheese? A disgusting sham.

In fact, all of Los Angeles was a sham. You couldn't go anywhere on foot. Not on your own. I spent my time sitting on the porch, thinking that I would never go anywhere definitively, that I was doomed to come and go, come and go, and that was the same as never having left. No, it was worse. Like the woman in Gustavo's story who opened a door, went into her house, killed her children and went out, not back into the street but into her house again and killed her children and went out, back into her house again, and so it went on, over and over. It was the worst story he had ever told me. During those days in Los Angeles, I thought that perhaps the time had come to invent my own formula for escaping myself, for killing my self-awareness with a bottle of pills.

The street looks like a mirror when it's wet, my nephew Simón said to me one day. He was sitting beside me on the porch, slouched, watching the rain falling on the road. The water made no sound when it fell, because the road was as smooth as an ice rink.

One day we all piled into my brother's truck and went to Universal Studios. We looked at it from outside because it was expensive to go in. Odina didn't even step out onto the pavement because her feet hurt.

Don't you ever go to school? I asked my nephew one morning when we were sitting on the porch. He shook his head.

Why not?

Because I'm ill.

I thought about the concoction my mother gave me. I

wondered what it was made of.

How old are you?

Five.

He looked about fifty, with that serious face of his.

What's wrong with you?

Asthma: he showed me his inhaler.

That's no excuse for not going to school, no sir, I told him, and he looked at me with his gigantic eyes, like two black billiard balls.

That afternoon we had a strawberry milkshake and some little guava cakes that his maternal grandmother had sent over from Puerto Rico. That evening, Simón told me he was scared of spiders. I told him a story:

Once upon a time there was a king...

What was the king's name?

Gustavo. He was a wise king who traded his kingdom for a shack in front of the sea.

Which sea?

The Caribbean Sea, you can't see it from here. Back in his kingdom he was rich and had a virgin wife for every night.

What for?

For every night.

And then I didn't know how to go on, because I didn't know that story, or any other stories, and Simón kept looking at me expectantly. What happened then? Nothing. Nothing?

I started over:

Once upon a time, there was a face...

A face? Simón laughed.

A face with big eyes, like black billiard balls. Above the face there was some hair, and under the face, a neck, and lower down, a little body that liked to slouch. And all of this made up a boy.

What was the boy called? Simón was looking at me as if this was a really great story; his laughter held back, a smile playing on his lips.

He was called Simón, and to get to sleep, he would count sheep backwards.

Backwards, like on their backs?

No backwards, like this: 100 little sheep, 99 little sheep, 98…

Didn't he know how to count?

Yes, but he counted in a different way.

Why?

I don't know.

14

I was on the last flight back from Los Angeles. The airport shops were already closed; the taxis rapidly filling up with tourists coming from Miami, where they caught their connecting flights. I walked to the apartment, which was six blocks away, dragging my heavy suitcase. When I arrived at the building, I sat down on the front step and lit a cigarette. As I stretched out my neck, I looked up, and was dazzled by the fried chicken sign. They had finally mended its beak.

I went up to the apartment. Milagros was staying with her French boyfriend, her message on the answering machine said. The French boyfriend was staying in a "boutique" hotel in town, a colonial mansion with only a handful of rooms… It's not often you get a chance to see those kinds of places, said Milagros, cheerfully, and the message ended. I cracked open a beer and leaned out of the window. There was no breeze. Then I watched a film about a woman who made it in New York as a bartender.

In the early hours of the morning, my mobile rang. Hello. It was the hospital: Gustavo had fallen and dislocated his hip, he would have to use crutches for a while. He needed someone to help him leave the hospital, take him home, wash him, give him something to eat. But I'm not a relative, I said. Do you know any of his relatives? No, they're all dead, they were thrown into the sea. Excuse me? said the nurse. I don't know of any relatives. We'll put him down as homeless. Okay.

But in the morning, I called the airline, extended my leave and went to the hospital. The nurse filled out a form which I had to sign so they could release him: Name and surname. Maritza Caballero. Relationship? Daughter. I took him back to his shack.

I'd brought him a Los Angeles Lakers cap. I put it on him. I asked him whether I should stay to look after him. He didn't say yes or no. He looked distant, bewildered. He didn't speak until dinner time, when he said, Do you like cloves? Me: not really. Round here people eat a lot of cloves, he said, and hauled himself into the tiny kitchen, took a couple of things out of the fridge and started cooking.

The days that followed went like this:

Gustavo would get up at five in the morning when it was still dark. He'd put on his cap, grab his crutches and fling open the door to the shack. In came the smell of salt and dead fish, which I found unbearable for the first few days. Then I got used to it. Anyway, I told him he really needed to get that pool emptied, that there was no longer any use for it, all he was growing in it was fungi, tadpoles, mould, decay. And that giant shapeless fish with the bulging forehead. It was a mutant fish, a sea monster capable of surviving in that black water, eating the leftovers that Gustavo chucked in there.

One morning I got up and the fish had mutated into a pig. It's not a pig, said Gustavo. But it looked like it. The fish was an enormous ball of pinkish flesh that opened its big gaping mouth when you went near it, like it was yawning.

Gustavo and I ate underneath the tarpaulin. Gustavo had stopped using the crutches after three days and had gone back to fishing. He was still wearing his cap. I went with him because he found it hard to walk, to move easily; he was quite lame. We went out at seven, in a rickety boat called *Everything is for you*. Why's it called that? I asked him.

Because it's true. We didn't do much fishing, but this didn't matter because Gustavo had no customers anymore. In the evening, at sunset, I would leave him cleaning the fish and go for a walk along the beach, to lie down on my back in the sand, and look at the sky.

Up and down, up and down, I touched myself, thinking about Tony. And about Tony's wife. And about his children's children, and his grandchildren's grandchildren. Lost causes, all of them.

Then I came back, and Gustavo had prepared some spicy, sickly stew. We ate some of it, then threw the rest into the pool for the pig-fish. Then we sparked up a joint. We lay in the hammock and watched the sky growing dark and filling up with stars, the moon, a handful of clouds. Gustavo told me stories that I already knew. Sometimes he told them wrong and I had to correct him. Sometimes he invented new, absurd, irrelevant parts. And I let him carry on. Until, one day, I stopped listening to him. It was easy, instead of hearing his voice assembling long, rambling sentences, I heard the sound of the waves and the wind: a cold, piercing howl that after a while, turned into a deafening hum. Then I focused on the horizon, which by that hour was empty.

PART II

WORSE THINGS

LIKE A PARIAH

That advert was on TV, the one with the fat guy who had lost weight by drinking some tea or other: *My son didn't want me to go to his football match and I asked him why – are you ashamed of me?* The former fatso cried and asked them to stop filming. They went on filming anyway. Inés always welled up at that commercial. She was not fat, had never been fat. But for some reason, this guy's story struck a nerve.

That morning she had tried to talk to Michel. Since the day of the move, she'd heard nothing from him. She'd dialled his number, but he didn't pick up. Maybe he was working. She had called him again just now, but still no answer. It wasn't even midday yet and she was exhausted, the previous night she had dreamt about her toes falling off. Lately, her feet hurt, and sometimes she felt as if they were gangrenous. It was a feeling like the one she had that time in Boston, when her legs had frozen up altogether. Michel was studying for his master's and she had gone to visit him; it was winter. The doctor there told her she had serious circulation problems. 'Like any damn highway, then!' replied Inés, trying to lighten the tone, but neither the doctor nor Michel laughed at her joke.

The ex-fatso had changed location and wardrobe. Now, wearing a black suit, he was posing on a balcony overlooking a city full of lights: *I hadn't seen my own penis for years.*

'Penis', mused Inés, 'what an ugly word.'

'Good morning, *señora*.' The cleaning woman was standing at the door to the study. She was wearing a dress buttoned up to the neck, even in that heat. Inés turned the TV off.

'Good morning...' she couldn't remember her name. It was only the second time she had ever seen her.

'Glenda, *señora*.'

Inés nodded. Glenda nodded too, came into the study and handed her an envelope that had been in the letterbox.

'Thanks.' Inés sat up, smoothed her hair with her hands. It felt rough, like a man's stubble.

'I'll be in the kitchen if you need anything.' Glenda turned and left. She was a large, dark-skinned woman with a very deep voice.

Inside the envelope was a card reading "Brunch". It was from the new occupants of the Las Palmeras condo and was addressed to Gerardo and her, using their full names. She wondered how they'd found out their surnames. They had barely been there a week.

She went out of the study, card in hand. She crossed the living room and opened the blinds, and the light burst into the room like a jet of water. She squinted. The workmen had just arrived; they had come to fix a rusted pipe. The garden stank. It was an old country house, passed down from an unmarried aunt of hers, and nobody in the family used it. Inés' sister had suggested that she move there temporarily, while she convalesced. Michel helped her move. Even Gerardo helped her. They all wanted her far away. 'It's cancer, not leprosy,' she had told them. They looked at her, offended.

She sat down on the sofa. If she went to the brunch, she would have to cover her head somehow.

On the small coffee table lay a copy of *Health!* magazine. Michel had brought her a few to keep her entertained; on the cover was an older woman, nibbling on some nuts like a squirrel.

She thought she should go to the brunch and meet her neighbours, after all, she was going to be living there for a while. A year. That's what she had told them all. Michel, Gerardo, her sister. She fanned herself with the magazine and looked outside: the workmen were slowly unpacking their tools.

'*Señora.*' It was Glenda. The magazine fell out of Inés' hands and onto the floor. The woman had appeared out of nowhere. 'Are you going to have breakfast?'

'No thank you.'

'Have you taken your medicines?'

'No, I'll do it later.' Inés ran her hands over her hair, picked up the magazine and put it on the table. Why did she have to ask her that?

'I think you should eat some breakfast, *señora*, you can't take those medicines on an empty stomach.'

'No, I don't want any.'

Glenda cleared her throat. 'Very well.' She turned around and wobbled through the kitchen.

Inés shook her head. She left the sofa and slowly climbed the stairs. She looked through her clothes to find something to wear.

A hat. She would have to wear a hat.

★

It was like something out of the movies, the stereotypical Californian condo. As if it belonged to a down-at-heel *mafioso*: curved balconies and tall palm trees planted symmetrically, one next to the other, forming a circle around an artificial lagoon. Then on each side, there were rows of houses, all identical, with their terraces out the

65

front. Inés was on one of these terraces, sitting in a wicker chair. A guy in white Bermuda shorts and a sky blue shirt had sat down next to her. He sipped his drink. In between the two chairs was a blue hat.

'Mother makes a fantastic fruit daiquiri,' said the guy. Inés nodded.

Mother? Who the hell talks like that?

The guy was called Leonardo and he must have been around forty. He worked in real estate, he had told her. The host was his mother, Susana, who was making her way towards them with two new colourful drinks. She held one out.

'Would you like another?'

Inés raised her face to look at her. Susana was silhouetted by the sun: a glowing halo surrounded her hair, which was dyed cherry red.

'Thanks.' She accepted the daiquiri, which, they had told her, was a blend of citrus juices. The doctor had told her she couldn't drink alcohol yet. 'Not even a small one?' Inés asked him. 'That's a bit mean.' Then he told her that she could have a small one, but that she shouldn't drink too much, because her body's defences were still low.

Susana sat on her son's lap, stirred her drink with the straw and downed it in one. Inés tried hers. It was far too sweet.

'Did Inés tell you where she lives, darling?' said Susana. Leonardo shook his head. 'In that house, the one that was falling down, but which now Inés and her husband, who works in...' Susana frowned and looked at her; she was wearing blue eyeliner. 'What exactly does your husband do?'

Inés looked down at her sickly-sweet drink. How could she answer that? One: he wasn't her husband anymore. Two: she had never understood what he did for a living. She never had an answer prepared, like most married women do. She'd heard those replies: it should never be a complete sentence like 'my husband works in...'; that was too vague and gave the impression that you needed too much time to think about something you should be able to reel off instantly. In those games of questions and answers, the way you formulated your answers could lose you valuable points: 'Crustaceans are animals that have the following characteristics...' It was a trap. The possible answers to Susana's question should be direct, short, efficient. 'What exactly does your husband do?' 'Soil mechanics' or 'Computing manuals' or even 'Acrylic fish tanks'.

Susana had turned to her son. 'Anyway, so Inés and her husband fixed up that house and it looks immaculate now. That's what they say. Isn't that right, Inés?'

Inés nodded. Who could possibly have said that?

She thought about the rotten pipe running through her garden. Then her mind replayed the ad of the ex-fatso crying: *I felt like a pariah.*

'...it's a very solid and attractive detached house, although...' Now it was Leonardo who was talking.

Inés sipped her drink; the cold liquid ran quickly down her throat and she wanted to cough but managed to control it. She suddenly felt poorly dressed: it was the hat, she must look like a real hick.

'...it has some problems with the pipework and electrics.' Leonardo was balding, and sweat accumulated each side of his widow's peak, out of reach of the handkerchief he used to wipe around his face every so often. The sweat glittered in the sunlight, making it look as if rays were emanating from his head. But he was not unattractive: he was tall, with blondish hair and one of those large, straight noses that give some guys an air of refinement. Michel had a small nose, but a lot of hair on his head.

'Having said that', Leonardo went on, 'I don't understand what made you move here, instead of finding a more comfortable option, given the circumstances.'

What circumstances?

Susana stood up abruptly and let out an idiotic laugh. She looked embarrassed by her son's question.

'Darling,' she said with her hand on her bust which, although drooping, was still rounded thanks to the implants. 'You can't ask Inés that, for God's sake.'

Susana was wearing flat sandals, blue, like her eyeliner, like the hat, like Leonardo's shirt. She must have been sixty-something. Inés was fifty-seven, but she felt about a hundred. She finished off the dregs of her drink. In the pool, a few people were floating around on lilos. Inés couldn't decide if she liked swimming pools or not. Gerardo hated them – *once you've dived in and had a splash about, then what do you do?*

Susana was still clumsily apologising for her son's indiscretion. Inés tried to focus on looking beyond the palm trees, which marked the course of the river, then disappeared out of sight down a sloping hillside. A waiter came up with a tray of daiquiris: this time there was also a whisky on there. Inés grabbed it. 'I think I'll move onto this.'

★

The verandah was the coolest part of the house, but it stank to high heaven. The builders were working out front, and the smell of the rotten pipes was overpowering. Glenda had come up with the idea of placing torches in the garden, and it worked quite well: she had wrapped stakes with rags soaked in citronella. The sweet, lemony oil repelled the mosquitos. She had soaked other cloths in jasmine essence and the resulting scent was penetrating and acidic, interspersed with occasional wafts of sickly-sweetness. A horrendous smell, but more bearable than the broken pipes.

That morning nobody had lit the torches yet. The workmen must have lost their sense of smell because there they were, sitting on the lawn, eating the bowls of food that Glenda had brought out to them, and breathing in that stench.

'Will you be taking lunch, *señora*?' Glenda startled her. She always did that. It was a mystery how a woman so huge could sidle right up to her without making a sound.

'Why haven't you lit the torches?' Inés asked.

'I'll light them now,' said Glenda. She always had a look of slight disgust on her face. 'Would you like me to serve you lunch?'

'What time is it?'

'One o'clock. Shall I serve up?'

'What did you cook?'

She huffed. 'Roast chicken and cornbread. That was all you had.'

'That's fine, thanks.'

'There's no food left, *señora*.'

'I'll tell Michel to do a shop for me.'

'This came for you.' Glenda took an envelope out of the front pocket of her apron and held it out. Inés opened it: it was another invitation from Susana. The following day she was having a get-together to celebrate the Day of Our Lady of Carmen. Glenda was still standing there, looking disdainful, her hand furtively covering her nose.

'What's wrong?' Inés asked her.

'Nothing.' Glenda went into the kitchen and immediately returned with a tray that must have been sitting there, ready to bring out. She put it down on the table: anaemic chicken with a congealed yellow mass next to it. It all looked cold and dry. Inés felt like she was going to throw up: she put a napkin to her mouth to cover the sound of the acidic belch that burned her throat. This had been happening to her since she had drunk those whiskies at the condo, a couple of days ago.

'I guess you know I won't be coming in until Tuesday, *señora*', said Glenda, who was still standing there, stiff as a corpse.

'What's that?'

'I'm not coming in, and I don't think the guys are either.' She gestured to the workmen. Inés pushed her plate away, nauseated.

'I don't understand what you're talking about. When aren't they coming?'

Glenda drew a deep breath.

'We won't be working Friday or Monday because it's the festival for the Virgin. And I was thinking…' She cleared her throat again.

'What were you thinking?'

'That you might like to ask your son to come and keep you company.' And off she went into the kitchen, without waiting for a reply.

Michel had called her the previous day. He didn't approve of her going to that party at the condo. 'It wasn't a party, it was a brunch,' Inés told him. And he replied, 'I can smell the fumes down the phone.' How dare he. She hung up. She didn't say anything; to avoid getting into an argument, she just hung up. He was getting more like Gerardo every day: bossy, judgemental. And she had become like a halfwit daughter to both of them.

She looked out into the garden again: the unlit torches, the workmen sitting on the ground, breathing in the stench. She was so tired. She made her way up to her room, but it was hard work: the stairs seemed steeper than usual.

★

It was too hot to have Gerardo on top of her. Inés pushed

him away and told him not now, later, when it was cooler. But Gerardo carried on crushing her with his sweaty body, with its sour smell. Inés bit his chest, tearing off a piece of flesh in her mouth, and still Gerardo didn't move. He was even stiller, lying there like a sandbag. Inés breathed slowly, inhaling the sliver of air between her face and Gerardo's bloodied chest. She started biting him again, stripping away more and more chunks of flesh until she reached his heart, an engorged bloody balloon that exploded as soon as she sank her teeth into it.

The noise woke her up: she opened her eyes. She was still on the sun lounger. She was forced to take a deep breath of the warm, reeking garden air, because she felt like she was suffocating. She touched her forehead with the back of her hand: she was freezing, but she felt hot inside. Her chest hurt, her feet hurt. Where had that noise come from? Next to the lounger was a bucket that had been full of ice. Now it didn't even have water in it; she had thrown it over herself before she fell asleep.

She had spent the entire day in just her knickers and bra, making the most of being on her own. She got up to fetch more ice and look for something to drink. She crossed the verandah, went into the kitchen and opened the fridge: there was only water in there. She took more ice out of the freezer and filled up the bucket. She went into the guest bathroom and peed, then got into the miniscule shower cubicle. Not even an insect could have showered comfortably in there, she thought. Dripping wet, she went to the kitchen, grabbed a dishcloth and dried her face. The cloth smelled of onions. She hurled it in the bin. She opened the larder, took a loaf of bread down off the shelf and smothered a slice in mayonnaise. It was the first thing she had eaten all day. She went outside and stood in front of the torn-up ground; the trench where they would lay

71

the pipe was the roofless hall of a giant mole's house. Not a sound could be heard except for the birds and, every so often, a bus beeping its horn in the distance. Inés went back to her lounger. She lay back and closed her eyes.

Again, the explosion.

When she opened her eyes, she saw coloured dots in the sky. It took her a few seconds to realise that they were fireworks. They were coming from the village. They were probably for the Virgin. A while later she heard the intercom buzz, it had a strange sound: muffled and nasal. It was one of those devices that were considered ultra-modern in the seventies. She stood up, crossed the verandah, went into the kitchen and glanced at the clock. Seven. The intercom buzzed again.

'Hello?' she answered.

'*Señora*, this is the watchman, I've got an envelope for you.'

'Okay,' her mouth felt furry. 'Please leave it in the letterbox.'

The man said he would. She waited for him to leave, went to the main gate and took the envelope out of the letterbox. It was a note from Susana, saying that she had been calling her on the phone, that she hadn't managed to reach her and that she mustn't miss the party that night, she would send a driver for her at eight o'clock, to make sure she came. Inés went into the living room and picked up the phone; the line was dead.

She took a shower. She put on her turquoise dress, which was nice and cool. She smoothed her hair down and wrapped her head in a silk scarf that Michel had given her. She slipped on some flat sandals, because her feet were so swollen that no other shoes would fit. Before she left, she picked up the phone to see if there was a dial tone. Nothing.

★

Someone was speaking to her from far away. And even further off, as if from behind glass, she could hear another voice:

'*I'd like to thank all the holes I ever stuck my cock in!*' It was Leonardo's friend. Inés turned her head and saw him standing on the diving board above the pool, naked, using a bottle as a microphone. '*Thank you for this award,*' now he held the bottle up in front of him with both hands, '*my ass is going to really enjoy it.*'

Inés touched her head. She no longer had her headscarf on. She felt dizzy.

'*Thank you to each and every one of the....*'

'So?' Now it was Leonardo, he was sitting on the floor, by her side. 'You were telling me about that fat guy who lost weight by drinking a tea. Is he a friend of yours?'

Inés' throat was dry, she couldn't get any words out. She felt a pain in her thigh. Leonardo was biting her. She pushed his head away feebly. She was naked, and so was he. Next to the sun-lounger was a side table with a bottle of whisky on it. It was almost empty.

'Where's my scarf?' She touched her head again.

'What did you say?' said Leonardo.

In the pool, someone was doing breaststroke.

'*Thanks to all the lips that have sucked me off...*'

'I can't feel my feet,' said Inés.

A little while ago, Inés, Leonardo and his friend had swum in the pool. Inés remembered that, and she remembered fingers pinching her nipples. She remembered thinking, maybe even saying it as well, that when their bodies rubbed together in the water, it did not feel real, as if they were wrapped in cling film. Now Leonardo's friend and Susana were in front of her, kissing. The guy had her headscarf wrapped around his dick: it was shrunken, purple, stuffed inside it like a stocking. Inés felt a burning sensation

73

inside her. She wanted to ask him to take her scarf off and give it back to her, but no words came out. The guy broke loose from Susana and reached for the whisky bottle on the table. He poured the dregs over Inés' breasts, and bent down to lick it off, but Leonardo stopped him.

'Leave her alone, can't you see she's totally out of it?'

The guy said something that Inés could not make out, and then leapt into the pool. Somewhere she could hear Susana laughing. Inés closed her eyes and felt something crushing her, so heavy that she could hardly breathe. She opened her eyes.

'Sshh, don't move.' Leonardo was straddling her belly. He wet his hand with his own spit and touched her down below. 'Your pussy's all dry and closed like an oyster.' He slipped a couple of fingers into her, jabbing so hard that one of his nails must have scratched her inside, because Inés could feel blood. A burning sensation.

'Please...' she mumbled.

She wanted to say something about her cancer, about her low defences.

She thought she had already told him.

Leonardo plunged his fingers in and out as if he were unclogging a drain; he jerked himself off with his other hand. He came with a loud moan, and slumped forward onto Inés, smearing his own semen under him.

*

The following day, Michel brought over the ingredients to make a lasagne. Inés served it at the table on the verandah. Michel cleared the leaves from the garden; he wielded the rake clumsily. The torches were lit.

'Lunch is ready, darling.' Inés felt groggy. She had a pounding headache.

Michel came over and poured Coke into two glasses with ice.

That morning, when she got back from the condo, Inés had got into the shower and stayed sitting there for several hours. Then Michel had arrived, making a fuss because she had not been picking up the phone. 'It's broken', Inés retorted. But when Michel went to check, he noticed that it was not broken, only unplugged. That put him in an even worse mood.

'You're not looking well,' he was saying now, chewing his food. 'Moving here was a bad idea.'

Inés gave a hollow laugh. 'But you were all so pleased about it!'

Michel pushed his plate away. 'You're unbearable, mother.'

Mother? He had never called her that before.

'Eat up', said Inés, 'it's getting cold.' She took a bite of the lasagne but could not swallow it.

'Where's the cleaning lady?'

Inés shrugged. 'She's not coming in until Tuesday.'

'Why?'

'Because of the Day of Our Lady.'

'Which Lady?'

'How should I know?'

They ate in silence. She was forcing down tiny mouthfuls. Her body hurt. Everything hurt. Soon the midges started bothering them, and Michel went to fan the flame of one of the garden torches, so the smoke would repel them. The putrid air wafting towards the verandah was replaced by the sweet smell of citronella.

Inés touched her breasts. They were throbbing. Michel was talking to her again:

'What have you been eating lately? The fridge was totally bare.'

'I know, that's why I asked you to do a shop for me. It's not easy to get out to the shops here.'

Michel finished off his plate and she helped him to a second serving. Her hands were shaking; she was shivering. She dried her sweat with the sleeve of her shirt. Michel was looking at her and this made her uncomfortable, as if he were scanning every bone in her battered body.

'Are you taking your pills?'

'Yes.'

'And the vitamins?'

'Yes.'

'Are you doing your stretches?'

'Every day.'

'Are you sure?'

'Yes, sir.'

Inés had given up on her food and was looking at the garden: the flame of one of the torches was flickering in the breeze, the smoke rising up from it in a curved, white line, which finally dissipated.

She wanted to smoke.

Once, halfway through her treatment, she had felt the same urge to have a cigarette. What made it even stranger was that she wasn't a smoker.

'It's a way of expressing your desire to die,' the doctor had said to her. 'And you are well within your rights to want to die.'

She was being sick all the time, she couldn't even keep water down. She was picking bloody scabs off her head.

Inés touched her head.

'Does it hurt?' said Michel.

'No, it's just that my hair's annoying me, it's itchy.'

'Put on that scarf I gave you... don't you like it?'

That time, near the end of her treatment, Michel and Gerardo waited for her outside the room. They had insisted on staying inside, but the doctor told them that there were some things that needed to be discussed with the patient alone. Inés said, 'Yes, the doctor's right,' and they looked at her like a couple of helpless little creatures.

'No, doctor, don't tell me that; I don't want to die.' And the doctor looked at her sadly, almost disappointed. 'How certain can you be, even with the treatment, that I am not going to die?' The doctor shrugged his shoulders in a gesture that seemed to her the height of cruelty. And she thought, 'Would it really be so hard for him to lie to me, just a little?'

Michel took a large mouthful of lasagne.

'You don't look at all well, mum,' he said, chewing again. He swallowed slowly, and repeated, sternly, 'Not at all well.' He looked away from her, his eyes shining, bitter.

Inés clenched her fist and banged it on the table.

'Oh, for God's sake!' she cried. 'I'm perfectly alright.'

YOU ARE HERE

Behind the reception desk was a sign reading: 'Welcome to the biggest hotel in Europe'. The ashtrays said the same thing, and so did the porter who had opened the door of the shuttle bus.

'Welcome to the biggest hotel in Europe,' he had said, gesturing grandly towards the building.

'Thanks, that's very kind,' said Pedro. He fumbled in his pockets. 'Sorry, I don't have any change.'

The woman at reception told him he should go to dinner straight away.

'I'd rather take my bag up to my room and have a wash, I'm pretty tired.' He felt ridiculous explaining himself to her. In any case, the woman didn't appear to be listening. She was shaking her head.

'You're in room 1439. By the time you've gone up and done all that, the restaurant will be closed.'

'Isn't there a lift?'

'I'd suggest you go to dinner right now.'

Spaniards certainly have an abrupt way of speaking, thought Pedro, dragging his heavy suitcase along the corridor the woman had pointed to. It seemed endless, with golden columns along each side and a shiny marble floor. He realised he'd forgotten to call Jimena before he left for the airport, as he'd promised. And now she would be worried, because she was neurotic like that. Hopefully it wouldn't occur to her to turn on the news: Madrid airport had come to a standstill because of an accident. No planes were taking off for the next twelve hours. The passengers would be shunted to this hotel. 'Was anyone killed?' Pedro had asked a flight attendant who seemed very on-the-ball during the evacuation. 'I can't give you that information,' she replied. She didn't need to, her tone revealed that yes, they were. Probably many people.

Years ago, before the children were born, Pedro and Jimena saw a dead body on the highway. They were in her mother's car, on the way to visit some friends at their farmhouse. Jimena started crying hysterically, and he had to pull over, shake her by the shoulders and give her a couple of hard slaps. Pedro never mentioned the episode again, but for some time afterwards, he could not get the image of the dead man's pale face out of his head, the face tight and swollen as if an air hose had been placed in his mouth and it had been inflated.

Halfway down the corridor, on the way to the restaurant, there was a circular atrium with a fountain in the middle, overlooked by some balconies. Pedro stopped next to the fountain and looked up. There was an opening in the roof revealing the sky above.

'*Señor?*' A few yards ahead of him a man in chef's whites was ushering him into the dining room. 'Will you be having dinner?' he said, wiping his face with a handkerchief.

'Yes.'

The passengers were lined up in front of a buffet, vouchers in hand, looking weary. All the food was creamy. Even the vegetables were swathed in a whitish dressing that congealed as soon as it landed on the plate, acquiring a yoghurt-like texture. Pedro helped himself to some sautéed broad beans and a glass of white wine.

The dining room was huge, but only part of it was laid

up. There were places to sit at two tables: one with two young women on it and another with a skinny guy who was shovelling down his food, his nose practically touching his plate. Pedro went for him. The girls seemed nice, but it wasn't worth the risk. After a while they would probably end up despising him, and he preferred to avoid that awkward moment when they pretended to continue to tolerate this flabby forty-something guy, with his bulky suitcase and his unfunny comments.

The skinny guy polished off everything on his plate and went up for seconds. Pedro barely touched his beans; he asked the waiter to refill his glass of wine several times. The guy was from Ecuador, he had come to Spain to attend a course in a town somewhere in Aragon, he couldn't remember the name of the place. The course had been terrible, but he had really liked the women.

'I do pretty well with European women,' he said, through a mouthful of bland-looking puree, though Pedro found this hard to believe. 'They're more direct.'

Pedro nodded.

'...and I know what I want in a woman,' said the Ecuadorian, making a hand gesture at the same time, like a fish swimming forwards. Pedro had no idea what it was supposed to mean.

'Do you smoke?' Pedro asked him, once the restaurant was almost empty and it appeared that the guy could not stuff any more food in. He wanted to get out of there, to go back to the round place with the opening in the ceiling. He wanted to smoke a cigarette.

The Ecuadorian downed the rest of his glass of Coke and they made their way out; Pedro with his heavy suitcase, and his companion with a woven travel bag slung over his shoulder. The corridor was as empty as it had been an hour before. Just across from the restaurant was another open door: shards of light reflected out into the hallway, the glimmer of a disco ball. They peered inside and the guy at the bar acknowledged them with a nod of the head. The chef from the restaurant was the sole customer.

'Shall we have a drink?' the Ecuadorian asked. Pedro said he'd prefer to go and smoke in the place he mentioned before, but the Ecuadorian went inside anyway. Pedro followed him. They sat down at the bar next to the chef and ordered two gin and tonics. Pedro placed a cigarette between his lips, hunted for his lighter in the pockets of his jacket and trousers, but couldn't find it.

'Have you got a light?'

The Ecuadorian said he didn't. Pedro looked at the barman and the guy shook his head.

'You can't smoke in here.'

Pedro stared at him. He looked like an Arab. He thought it was bad form to let them order their drinks before telling him that. It was blatantly obvious he was planning to smoke: he was holding the packet in his hand, he looked on edge, they had taken him off a plane because there were dead bodies strewn over the runway, and they had given him some vouchers to eat that mush that passed for food. The Ecuadorian got up from the bar and went to put some music on, at a machine that was supposed to look like a jukebox, but which was actually just a computer. Pedro turned to the chef, who was swirling his drink around in his glass.

'Do you mind if I smoke?'

The chef looked at the barman and the barman shook his head.

'You can't.'

The chef shrugged. Pedro clutched his head. He wanted to fall into bed and go to sleep. He wouldn't even unpack. Tomorrow morning, he'd shower and put on the same clothes and spend the day on the terrace, drinking sickly sweet cocktails with little paper umbrellas in them. In the evening he would go to the airport and fly home, to his bed, to sleep beside Jimena.

The glow of a lighter flame illuminated his face: the barman had taken pity on him.

'Just one, and if anyone comes, you put it out,' he said, with an accent that reminded Pedro of a soap opera his mother used to watch when he was young: *Renzo, the Gypsy*. He must be Andalusian, not Arab.

Pedro swung his bar stool round to face the dance floor and took a deep drag of his cigarette: he closed his eyes, holding in the smoke. When he opened his eyes, he saw the Ecuadorian dancing with one of the girls who had been in the restaurant. The chef was still sitting next to him.

'Did you see the accident?' the chef asked him, his voice slurred.

Pedro wondered how long the guy had been drinking for: less than an hour ago he'd been serving the buffet. Maybe he was always drunk. Maybe he spat in the food. Pedro shook his head.

'I heard a lot of people died,' said the chef.

'So they say.'

'How many?'

'I don't know.'

The chef knocked back the rest of his drink.

'So, what do you do?' he asked.

'I sell things.'

'What kind of things?'

Pedro shrugged. 'Appliances.'

'Household appliances?'

'Yeah, something like that.'

It had nothing to do with household appliances.

'Right.'

The chef topped up his glass from a bottle of vodka that the barman had left on the bar a few minutes ago.

'So, is this really the biggest hotel in Europe?' Pedro asked him, and the chef raised his eyebrows, nodding vigorously.

At one end of the bar, the barman was chatting up the other girl, the friend of the one dancing with the Ecuadorian. They looked Dominican, or something like that: dark-skinned, ample-bottomed. A song was playing that seemed completely out of place in the soulless atmosphere of the bar: *Your dark eyes in the sunshine, light up your smile.*

'Is it ever full?' asked Pedro.

The chef shook his head doubtfully. Then he frowned.

'Is *what* ever full?'

'The hotel.'

'Oh yeah, when there are conferences.'

'Sure.'

'And all the businessmen and hostesses come.' The chef made a gesture of licking his lips. Just then, the Ecuadorian appeared. The girl he was dancing with had gone to the toilet.

'Are the hostesses European?' asked the Ecuadorian.

'Sometimes,' replied the chef.

'Ufff,' said the Ecuadorian, as if a hostess were there right now, on her knees in front of him.

'…sometimes they are Asian.'

The Ecuadorian shook his head.

'I don't like that type.'

Pedro's leg had gone to sleep. He straightened up, putting one foot on the floor. It felt the same as it always did, but more intense: like tiny needles pricking his skin. The chef and the Ecuadorian went on talking about hostesses. Pedro thought about the people who died in the accident and he had an urge to hug his children. Hug all three of them so tight that they'd protest and push him away, gasping for air.

'Charge the drink to room 1439 please,' he told the barman, who waved him away, saying, 'Don't worry about it.'

*

They had told him to use the lift at the end of the corridor, and that he would have to walk the equivalent of two city blocks. Pedro stood at the door to the bar, looking at the enormous space in front of him. He could not imagine a convention that could fill that whole space. Perhaps three conventions at the same time might, though not if they were Asians, because they are so small. The opening through which the sky could be seen was behind him, in the opposite direction to the lift. Inside the bar, the Ecuadorian was saying something in the girl's ear and she was laughing. The barman had returned to his seat across from the chef and the other girl had disappeared. He wondered what time it was.

'Excuse me,' came a voice from behind Pedro.

It was the barman's girl. She wanted to leave the bar, but he and his suitcase were blocking her way. He moved aside, and the girl stepped out into the corridor.

'What've you got in there, a dead body?' She laughed.

Pedro forced a smile. 'Appliances,' he replied, 'I sell appliances for...' There was no point explaining; nobody understood anyway.

'Cool.' She stood there in front of him.

She was young, and not exactly a looker. She could have been pretty if her cheeks hadn't been covered in acne scars.

'Do you smoke?' Pedro asked her.

She nodded. He told her that there was an opening where you could see the sky, that it was back there – he pointed – and asked if she wanted to go there and smoke a cigarette. She said she did.

★

The girl's name was Rosario and she wasn't Dominican. She didn't say where she was from: the Caribbean, in any case. She didn't ask where he was from either, only saying, 'Here in Europe it's all the same.' Pedro told her that it was his first time in Spain and that he'd hardly left the hotel. He had come to attend some company training, which was being held right there, where he was staying.

'It's better like that,' said Rosario. Pedro nodded, but didn't understand what she meant. He didn't mind staying in the hotel, he told her, he wasn't a very curious kind of guy. He liked the simple things: peace and quiet, sleeping well, eating well.

'When I travel, I always have issues with the food, my stomach gives me a lot of problems.' He was talking too much, it must have been the wine, the gin and tonic. Rosario laughed, revealing an abundance of large, white teeth.

The opening in the roof was a black circle. The fountain was turned off and they had to speak quietly because there was a slight echo. Before, when they got there, they had sat down next to one another, leaning their backs against the fountain. Pedro took out his cigarettes but then remembered that he didn't have a lighter. Rosario lay on the floor, her hair spread out above her head like a halo of curls. Pedro lay down next to her.

'At the training,' he was saying to her now, 'one of the guys showed us a black circle on a screen and zoomed right in so we could see the state of the pixels.'

'Why did he do that?'

Because images lost their clarity when the pixels died.

At the training, there were discussions about dead pixels and stuck pixels, which were not dead, but which were almost impossible to fix. Stuck pixels were in limbo inside the black circle, red, shining.

'I dunno,' said Pedro. He didn't want the conversation getting too technical.

'OK,' said Rosario. Then she added, 'There's no moon tonight.'

'No.'

Rosario pointed to the black opening.

'But I think I can see a star.'

There was nothing there.

Pedro smelled the sweat of her underarms and got a slight erection. He had heard that mixed-race women sweated more than white women. Jimena was as white as a sheet of paper, and had blue veins running over her body like circuit boards. And she did not have a scent. Though sometimes she had a stale smell about her.

His erection had gone.

'The guy who's with Vivian,' said Rosario, 'is he your friend?'

'Vivian?'

'My friend.'

'Oh, no, we're not friends. I met him just now, in the restaurant.'

'He's a creep.'

Pedro didn't know what to say to that.

He was thinking about dead people again. He had not seen the bodies. His plane was evacuated quickly; nobody explained what was going on. Outside, they heard about the accident and a woman started crying, screaming, and he remembered the dead body on the motorway, remembered Jimena. Someone asked if the screaming woman knew someone on the plane involved in the accident, but she didn't, she was just upset by it. The image of so many dead bodies on the runway, the night falling around them and all the sirens wailing outside; it must have all been too much for her.

'Are you scared of dying?' Rosario asked him, as if reading his mind.

'No,' he replied, perhaps too quickly.

Rosario stretched out on the floor, and the odour of her armpits intensified.

'Me neither. They say that death happens in less than a second, you can't be scared of something as brief as that!'

Pedro found this funny.

'Vivian: she's afraid of death, and she's convinced that today we were very close to dying. That's why she's with that idiot friend of yours.'

'No, he's not my friend, I mean...'

'Oh, don't make excuses for him, you must be thinking the same thing, but you don't dare say it.'

'Say what?' Pedro was losing track. He wanted to smoke. He didn't have a light.

'You guys are all the same. You act the big man, and then something happens and you shit your pants, and all you want is a woman to lick them clean for you.' Rosario laughed.

'What?' Pedro looked at her again. She was sitting up now, her jeans clung tightly to her hips, and some flesh bulged out at the sides.

'Why don't you just ask me directly? Why not save yourself the bother of the whole story about the opening in the roof, the sky and the cigarette?'

'I don't know what you want me to...'

'Come here.' Rosario placed a hand on the back of his neck and pulled him towards her.

*

Pedro had muted the volume on the news, which was replaying images of the accident. It showed bodies on the runway, covered in white sheets, and the stretchers whisking them away as if they were props. Rosario was asleep next to him, naked: her bare flesh was much more attractive out of the jeans. Pedro was particularly interested in the crease of her waist: a line in her skin like the slot of a piggy bank. A while ago he would have sworn that Rosario was one of those plump women who, when they wore certain clothing, men would fantasise about taking it off, but then find the result to be disappointing. She had not been much of a disappointment, however. Or perhaps she just looked good lying down. Rosario opened her eyes, and they met his as he was scrutinising her. She made no move to cover herself up.

'What're you doing?' she said with a smile.

Pedro looked back at the screen. A reporter was saying something, but he couldn't hear what.

'What were you looking at?' said Rosario. And almost immediately, 'I didn't hear what you said.'

'I didn't say anything.'

'Were you watching the news?' she insisted.

Pedro changed the channel several times until he landed on one where nothing was happening: snow.

'Are those pixels?' Rosario asked.

'No.'

'They look like pixels.'

The conversation was boring him.

'…I would've said those were pixels.' Rosario put her hand on his leg and stroked it. Pedro felt uncomfortable. Why hadn't they gone to her room instead? Then all he would have to do was leave. He had left his suitcase downstairs, propped against the fountain.

'What is it that you sell?'

Why couldn't she just be quiet? He liked Rosario when she was asleep, and even then, not that much.

'Pixels die,' said Pedro.

'Oh yeah?' She rolled over onto her front, hugging a pillow, feigning interest. Pedro placed his open hand on the cheek of her bare bottom. It was warm. He pinched it and she slapped his hand away.

'Hey!' She pulled the sheet over herself.

Earlier, Pedro hadn't come. He had just watched Rosario's movements on top of him, as he lay on his back, right at the edge of the bed. Rosario kept one foot on the floor and grabbed the headboard. She'd made the usual circular movement with her hips, as if she were kneading something, or moulding a piece of clay.

Pedro got up off the bed, located his trousers on the floor and started to pull them on. He thought he really should go and get his suitcase. He felt tired, impatient, he wanted to shower, to call Jimena. Rosario had lit a cigarette. On the bedside table there was a box of matches, with a small map of the hotel drawn on it, and a cross showing the location of the hotel: *You are here.* This had made him anxious: being there, underneath that cross, in such a vast and strange place. Stuck.

'Want some?' Rosario held out her cigarette.

Pedro stopped getting dressed and took it. He went to the window and opened the curtains. The window had a view of a large internal courtyard connecting their building to another one, and beyond that, slightly to the left, there was another one, and then another one, and so on: a succession of buildings forming a semicircle.

You are here.

So where was everyone else?

'What does a dead pixel look like?' asked Rosario.

Pedro turned around to look at her, but she was nowhere to be seen. She had turned off the TV and the room was in darkness, except for the corner with the window. He looked back out at the enormous courtyard and took a drag of the cigarette.

'It's a red dot on a black background.'

WORSE THINGS

Titi was called Ernesto, after his maternal uncle, who was like a father to him. Titi's dad lived in another city with his other family, but he came to visit him every couple of weeks. It was not far, the city, only an hour by car, and his dad had a really fast car. Titi used to wait for him on the pavement outside his house, dressed in dark jeans and a long-sleeved shirt, which made him hot. His mum liked to dress him like that when his dad came. Standing on the pavement, Titi could hear the roar of the engine from streets away; and a few seconds later, there was a screeching sound and a cloud of yellow dust was thrown up, covering everything.

In his head – as he used to explain it to himself, or sometimes to his uncle Ernesto – Titi liked seeing his dad, but in real life he didn't enjoy his visits. They didn't have much in common. Titi's dad, who was called Daniel, was an athletic guy. He played all kinds of sports and jogged every morning with a group of people who ran in those marathons sponsored by sports brands. Titi hadn't inherited a single one of those genes. He was an anomaly: his mum, whose name was Fanny, was not as athletic as his dad, but she was slender as a willow: that's what her friends from book club, who met every Tuesday at their house, used to say. Every time they said that, she glanced sideways at Titi, who pretended to be watching TV, lying on the floor belly-up, like a baby mammoth. Then she would gesture to her friends, using hand signals, to kindly change the subject.

'You were born that way, my love, there's nothing we can do to change that,' his mum explained, the first time Titi asked her why he was so fat.

Titi had been born uncommonly overweight, and his condition, according to the doctors, couldn't be treated early on. At first, Fanny did not see much of a problem with her baby being fat; on the contrary, she saw it as a sign of good health. Daniel, on the other hand, insisted that they put him on a diet and go to see a nutrition specialist.

'Do you want him to have liposuction?' Fanny said to him, 'Do you want your son to look as scrawny as that tart of yours?'

By that time, Titi's dad was already living with his lover. She was just like him: athletic. She was also much younger than Fanny and worked for a big multinational, instead of in a public library. When Titi was five years old a little sister arrived, who at the age of six months was winning crawling races at her nursery; by nine months she was walking and by fourteen months she could run as fast as a hare. At least that's what his dad told him; he'd had T-shirts made with a photo of the little girl clutching a trophy shaped like a baby bottle, which read 'I'm speedy'. When Titi put the T-shirt on, his little sister's face stretched out at the sides. He did not wear it very often, because as soon as Fanny spotted it in the laundry basket, she started using it as a cleaning cloth.

His dad spent a good part of their evenings together trying to convince him that he should take up a sport or that, at least, every morning he should go for a walk around the block.

'On the first day, walk to the corner and back. Then increase it to the next block, and that way, every day you'll be setting yourself new goals.'

Titi listened to him attentively, looking straight ahead,

as he sucked on the straw of his sugar-free fruit juice, which was the only thing his dad allowed him to drink when they were together.

'Will you do it, my boy?' he asked, finally, with a look of desolation that made Titi nod enthusiastically, although he knew he would never do anything of the sort; he couldn't do it, because of his respiratory insufficiency. He thought it was odd that his father didn't know that, but he didn't feel like explaining it to him either.

★

There was a period when Titi's classmates used to sneak up on him; they would move gradually closer to him, and then, all of a sudden, they would stab him in the belly with sharpened pencils, to see if he would deflate. Sometimes they drew blood, and that was serious, because Titi had a blood clotting disorder. He would then run, with difficulty, to the sick bay, so they could treat him and call his mum or his uncle. The children played other jokes on him: like filling his desk with leftover food. They normally did that last thing on a Friday, so when Titi came back to school on Monday he would find a cloud of bees and flies swarming above his desk, which was stuffed with rotting food. That's why he never left his schoolbooks in there. He carried all of them with him, every day, even though it made his back ache. Fortunately, his uncle Ernesto dropped him off at school every morning and picked him up every afternoon and helped him carry his schoolbag. But during the day, Titi could be seen plodding along, hauling that mass of books on his back like a huge turtle shell, his face greasy with sweat. Some of his female teachers invited him to sit and eat with them, so he could put his bag down and rest for a while.

When Titi turned twelve, he stopped wearing jeans. He no longer fitted into the largest children's size, or even a small adult size. He was embarrassed to wear a medium adult size. 'Embarrassed in front of who?' screeched Fanny, and Titi looked at the saleswoman and shrugged. They went for cotton tracksuits in the end. Around that time, uncle Ernesto said that Titi should be given a little more independence: at twelve years old, all the boys went to and from school on the bus or by bike. Whereas Titi, with her permission, had only gone on his own a few times. Fanny was against the idea. Firstly, because Titi didn't fit into the bus seats and, instead of being understanding and caring, people jostled him out of the way, forcing the boy to sit on the back step like a grubby piece of luggage. From there he couldn't see his stop and ended up missing it. Titi didn't find it that bad: sitting there, he could look up the women's skirts and see their knickers. He liked that. Secondly, Titi's bike was too cumbersome and he had never learned to ride it very well. He could fall and graze himself, and God forbid – said Fanny, her chin trembling – bleed to death before the ambulance arrived.

The subject was never broached again.

'How was your day, champ?' Lately his uncle had taken to calling him champ, and Titi didn't like it. It was obvious that he was not, and would never be, a champion at anything and it seemed insulting for someone to call him that. Titi shrugged and grunted something incomprehensible at his uncle in response.

'It's just adolescence,' Fanny said, when her brother told her that Titi was behaving oddly: sullen, introverted. Fanny was annoyed by the excessive attention people paid to her son's shortcomings: as if everything he did was related to his weight. And no, Fanny said to herself, some things just weren't. Ernesto did not go on about it, but he felt bothered by it, uncomfortable. Because as he was growing up, Titi was becoming more and more absent as a person. He spent hours with his eyes glued to a videogame that involved hunting people with an enormous net, which self-generated from phlegm hawked up by the player: an avatar designed by Titi, in the image and likeness of Titi himself.

*

'His condition prevents him from socialising normally; he spends more time in the sick bay than in the classroom.' The teacher was talking in a way Fanny found phony.

'It can't be all that bad,' said Fanny.

Daniel, sitting next to her, looked at her as if he had only just noticed she was there.

Titi was now fourteen and weighed seventeen stone. They had discovered a new problem: he was allergic. He wasn't allergic to anything in particular, he was just allergic. Every so often, bumps would appear all over his skin. They were incredibly itchy and could only be controlled with an expensive injection.

'And what would you recommend we do then, Miss?' said Daniel, frowning, looking at the teacher with a gesture that sought to express concern, but which Fanny knew was lechery, plain and simple.

'I would say that he needs a special school', said the teacher, and Fanny felt as if she had been slapped in the face. She looked at Daniel, who was pensive: his forehead creased into three deep, straight lines. Fanny imagined that he was thinking of all the things he could do to the teacher with his tongue. The man was obsessed with tongues. It had been years, but she remembered perfectly. She stood up from her chair and breathed deeply, pressed her forefinger between her brows and moved it in circles.

'Are you feeling alright?' asked the teacher.

'What you're saying is unacceptable,' she replied, 'Do you know I can have you done for discrimination? They can't throw Titi out of the school for being fat.'

'It's not that, Fanny, it's…' Daniel started to speak, but Fanny grabbed her handbag and left the room, the school, the block, the neighbourhood, and walked all the way home.

This time, Ernesto was on her side:

'No way.'

Titi was in the room. 'I want to go to a special needs school,' he said, without looking up from his videogame. Fanny looked at him, forlorn. 'But you're not "special needs".' Her shoulders, which were normally upright and straight as a clothes hanger, slumped down. Ernesto looked down at the floor. Titi jabbed at the "shoot" button and killed three victims. He looked up and said to his mother, 'Then I don't want to go to any school.'

★

'Your son isn't special,' said the headmaster of the special needs school, and Fanny clenched her fists.

'Of course he's special, didn't you see him? I can spend hours reeling off all the illnesses he suffers from because of his obesity. Or perhaps it's the other way around: the obesity is a symptom of the many deficiencies of his body. Although we'll never know for sure.'

That day, Titi was wearing a pair of baggy grey trousers and a very wide-fitting cotton shirt; his mum had sent him to a local seamstress to get it made. He was a little Buddha. Fanny thought that by exaggerating his size, he would be taken more seriously. Titi waited outside the headmaster's office with his uncle Ernesto, who was praising the school's wide-open spaces, and leafy gardens, and the chemistry lab with those little foetuses in jars of formaldehyde, as Titi reached the final level of his game. When he was engrossed in his game, Titi looked like he was in a trance: his pupils over-dilated, the vessels pumping blood into the yellowish cornea and the rest of his face distended. His jaw would slacken, letting whatever was in his mouth slide out. Drool, mostly.

'Let's go.' Fanny came striding out of the headmaster's office.

Ernesto jumped up. 'So? When do classes start?'

'Never.'

★

By sixteen, he could only wear kimonos. His obesity, they found out, was progressive and by that point, uncontrollable. Over time he would deteriorate. First his motor functions and then his internal organs. It was difficult to predict how fast this would happen. For the moment, the hardest thing was walking, so they decided to limit that as much as possible. A nurse assisted him from nine o'clock to five o'clock, when Fanny arrived home and took over. In any case, Titi did not do much apart from playing on his computer, which was set up with controllers on a table in front of the bed; eating the small amounts of grains, soups and porridges that his diet permitted; and walking to the bathroom.

'How's my brave prince?' When Fanny arrived home, the first thing she did was go to Titi's room. She always found him in the same position; hunched over, mouth open, eyes fixed on the computer.

'Did you have a good day?'

'Great, mum, I had a fabulous day,' he replied, sarcastically.

'Do you want to play Monopoly?'

'No.'

'Ludo?'

'No.'

Titi had advanced a lot with his video games; he now had a programme which enabled him to modify the initial design. Now the virtual Titi no longer hawked up phlegm, but instead carried a weapon that fired out children's heads that burst open when they hit the target. The city he was moving around was made of rubble and human remains. The main street was paved with bones that crunched when he stepped on them.

'Cards?'

'...'

At nine o'clock on the dot, his father would call. They saw each other very little: Daniel was very busy at work. It was a new job that, he told Titi, involved shouting at loads of useless people.

'Tell me what you've been up to, my boy.'

'I don't have anything to tell you.'

Titi tried not to lose his patience or concentration on the game: this was the time of day when he was at his best. In the mornings he woke up in a bad mood; after lunch he was sleepy: after his afternoon nap it was too hot. None of this helped him improve his high score. In the evening his mother came home, fussing over him, then his uncle would show up, looking all miserable, and just when they finally left him alone, his dad would call. All Titi wanted, for once in the day, was to clutch the controller and fire off those children's heads.

★

'Are you sure?' Daniel's voice wavered.

'The doctor mentioned an alternative treatment,

something experimental that they do in the States...' Fanny was crying, whispering into the kitchen phone, while she kept an eye on the corridor, as if there was a possibility that Titi might get out of bed to come and spy on her.

'If we have to take him there, we take him there.' Sometimes Daniel adopted optimistic airs that Fanny detested. 'Did the doctor say how much the whole treatment would cost?'

'No.'

'Will it stop the deterioration?'

'No.'

'So?'

'It can lengthen...' Fanny was choking on her tears.

'It can what?'

Fanny hung up. She ran the tap and splashed her face with water. She made her way to Titi's room and went in.

★

'No,' said Titi, cutting her off.

'But, darling, it's a simple treatment, very safe. You'll be able to do so many things that...'

Titi did not even look at her, did not notice the seriousness of her voice. He was engrossed in the screen. And in his cough. It was a new symptom of his respiratory failure: one of the most dangerous, because if he coughed up phlegm, he could suffocate. That's why it was better for him to stay sitting up.

The air in the room was so thick with various odours that Fanny felt sick. She sat down on the corner of the bed, wept silently, wringing her hands. On the screen, she saw the avatar's face, which was just like Titi's but covered with scars. It had webbed feet, claws for hands, and long tits, like tongues hanging down to its knees.

'You don't have tits, Titi,' she told him, in a tone that sounded more like a question than an affirmation.

★

'Does Titi have tits?' Fanny asked Ernesto a few nights later, as they sat drinking herbal tea after dinner.

'What?'

'I reckon he thinks he has tits.'

'He doesn't have tits.'

'That's what I said.'

They both took a sip from their mugs. They both thought that there wasn't much more to say on the matter. It wasn't something that was up for debate: does Titi have tits? Yes or no? No. That's what they'd said, and that was that.

★

'I need to shit,' said Titi.

For a few months, he had been looked after by a beefy male nurse, because the previous female nurse could no longer handle his weight.

'What did you say?' he asked, bringing his ear close to Titi's mouth because his voice had weakened. Or not exactly: the disease had caused the body to gain weight, but some of the internal organs had remained the same size and were therefore insufficient. On an X-ray, it was possible to see how his vocal cords were lost within the immensity of his vocal apparatus. 'He has the voice box of an elephant, with the capacity of a mosquito,' was how Fanny had explained it once.

The nurse sat him on the toilet, half closed the door and waited outside.

'Finished,' said Titi after a while, and the nurse went in.

By that time, Titi had grown bored of his game. He could no longer move his thumbs very well. Also, he told the male nurse one afternoon, he had already smashed all the possible high scores. He had started playing against other players online and had beaten them. There were only a few of them: his game was so "customised" that nobody seemed to like it as much as he did. Even he grew to dislike it. One day, the virtual Titi let himself get killed by some flying children who fired acid out of their navels, and he did not regenerate. That was the day he discovered the window.

'I want to go out.'

'What did you say?'

When he understood what Titi was saying, the nurse was speechless. After a moment he said, 'I'll check with your mum.'

Fanny thought that Titi would be too embarrassed in front of the neighbours. So would she. She thought it was better not to make things more complicated than they were; this was what life had given them, and things were fine. Relatively fine. What could be worse? So many things. *There were worse things.*

She looked into her son's expectant eyes.

'I think it's a great idea.'

'Me too,' said Ernesto.

The nurse nodded.

It took three days to arrange the outing. One Friday, at around eleven o'clock, in a wheelchair that the nurse had borrowed, they took him out to a nearby park at a time when it wouldn't be very busy. After a week, it became a routine outing. Daniel took days off work and came to pick them up: off they went, Ernesto, the nurse and Titi in front. When they reached the park, they would lower him out of the chair, sit him on the grass, his back leaning against a stone bench. If Fanny had found out about that, she might have put a stop to the outings on account of his allergy, but none of them said anything to Fanny. The three men sat near Titi, shielding him from the dogs, and the kids, and the balls flying through the air. They sipped beers, making jokes, talking about women: they threatened to take Titi to a brothel. They laughed. Titi nodded, didn't say much, smiled more for their sake than for his. Then he would say, 'My back hurts,' and they'd help him lie down on his back, with his head propped up on a cushion, in case he coughed up phlegm. Lying there, he stopped listening to them. He watched the clouds slowly crawling by; he wondered if they were coming or going. And where to. Hours passed, days passed, clouds passed and Titi wished that one would stop and furiously empty itself onto him. Until he was swept away; until there was nothing left.

BETTER THAN ME

'I've thought about it', said Becky over the phone, 'and it's not really a good time.'

The previous day, Orestes had told her he wanted to come and visit. She said no, she had a lot of work to do. He insisted, 'Please think about it.' And she had thought about it, she was telling him.

'Rebecca, please.' Becky hated being called Rebecca. As soon as he said it, Orestes regretted it. 'There's not going to be another chance: your mum and I don't have the money to travel, I came especially to this conference because…'

'I don't want to see you,' said Becky in a flat voice.

Orestes was attending a week-long conference on education in the age of the internet, in a small town near Rome, where Becky lived.

'But why not?'

'You're having a crisis and I'm not good at dealing with crises.'

'But I want to see you. You're my daughter.'

'I don't see how those two things are related.'

'I'm coming, and that's final.'

Becky sighed.

The conference was at a university that was very different to his own – there was no graffiti on the walls, no grimy hallways – but Orestes was not interested in the conference. He did not even know what it was about. He had asked around his colleagues about conferences in Italy and signed up for the cheapest one. He told the dean that if they sent him to that conference, he would progress up the academic ladder and this would help both the university and him. This was not true, he needed much more than a conference to climb the ladder, and in any case, there would be no point him climbing the ladder because in a few months he would be retiring. The dean looked at him in silence, his hands folded on the desk. Orestes told him that it was free and that the participants would be put up in university residences. He just needed the air fare. This was not true either: he was going to use some of his savings to pay the registration fee and for the accommodation in a student residence that was far from glamorous. The dean slowly shook his head. He picked up the phone and asked his secretary to arrange the trip.

'Darling?'

Becky was silent, but he could hear an irritating noise over the phone. Like marbles rolling around on a glass table, thought Orestes.

'Okay,' she said finally. The noise stopped.

Orestes gulped.

'So, I can come?'

'I'm not going to be there, but I can leave the key under the front door mat. There's a microwave, some things in the freezer...'

'Where are you going? Rebecca, don't be silly.'

'...there's a theatre in the neighbourhood that puts on some interesting plays. I'll leave my membership card on the bedside table.'

'Becky.'

'I have to go.'

She hung up.

A year earlier, Orestes' youngest daughter Rosa had suffered a nervous breakdown: she was a schizophrenic. Rosa had studied to be a teacher, like her dad, but just before her first interview with a secondary school, she had a breakdown. Orestes checked her into a hospital, where she lasted two months: one night she escaped from her room, went up to the roof and threw herself off. His wife had been traumatised by it and had not spoken to him since. They lived in the same house – a nurse helped her with everything – but they rarely saw one another.

Becky had lived in Rome for six years; Orestes did not understand what she did for a living, something to do with the stock exchange. In all that time, Becky had visited them a couple of times: first, when her mother broke her hip; and second, when Rosa killed herself. She stayed a week with them, and Orestes noticed how much she had changed. She looked unattractive, unkempt. Her face had a permanent sheen to it; she always wore her hair tied in a bun at the nape of her neck. She had become one of those pragmatic, diligent women. At the time, he did not think it was anything serious, because it had suited the circumstances: Becky quickly cleared out all her sister's clothes, rearranged the bedroom, removed her photos from the living room. Within a week it was as if Rosa had never existed. There was no trace left of her, except for her graduate thesis, which Orestes kept in the study and would not hand over, despite Becky's insistence: 'We mustn't give the ghosts anything to feed on.'

Rosa specialised in Piaget and her thesis analysed the egocentrism of the child. Orestes had read it many times and liked it. More than that: he thought it was brilliant. In his day, he had also written a brilliant thesis that the university had published. After that he had tried to write, but it would not come. He shut himself away in his cubicle, took out his notebook and transcribed his notes onto the computer. He typed slowly, and so the days went by. Two years later he had managed to finish a short essay, which he presented to the university publications department, but they did not want it. When they returned the manuscript, the editor in charge winked at him and said, 'Are you being funny, or trying to be clever?' He showed his horrible yellow-toothed smile. Orestes did not understand the joke, but days later he had an inkling. He hunted for the essay within his graduate thesis and found it there. Identical. It was an extract of a longer chapter. What did that mean? That he had gone mad? No, it meant that he had already used up all the ideas in his head, and all that was left was a permanent echo. He became depressed.

'It happens,' said a colleague who had published around twenty books. He sat down next to him on an old wooden bench at the university. 'Don't put pressure on yourself, read some crime novels, go to the cinema, grow some tomatoes on your balcony.' And he slapped him on the back.

Apart from the tomatoes, Orestes had done all of those things. He was still depressed.

*

'Becky? Please pick up.' Voicemail again. Orestes hung up and lay back on the bed.

The residence had low ceilings and the rooms were small and badly ventilated. Every time he moved around that room, he felt he was hopping about like a little bird.

That afternoon would be the first closing session of the conference, but Orestes was not going. A colleague from the faculty had put him in touch with a friend of hers who lived in a nearby town: 'You're going to get on so well,' she insisted. That evening he was going to meet her at a roadside diner. He would take the train. He didn't really feel like going, but he didn't feel like staying in either.

★

'But why do they hate you?' The woman was called Yara and worked for a body at the United Nations. A voluminous afro surrounded her head.

Orestes shrugged. He didn't feel like explaining.

Yara ordered pasta with a strongly flavoured, pungent sauce. Orestes did not order anything to eat, only wine. He had just told her that sometimes he imagined not going home.

'Perhaps you just need some "time off".' Yara was Venezuelan, but her language was littered with English words because she had studied in the United States. 'Perhaps it's *you* who hates *them*, and they can sense it.'

Orestes shook his head. Then he told her that Becky made him feel something that was akin to the pain of a distant death. Not the death of someone close: he already knew what that felt like. The other, distant kind, was more like a feeling of over-tiredness that paralyzed him. Yara listened to all of this as if she was genuinely interested: they had been sitting there for three hours, so she could only have been bored stiff, or drunk.

'And what would you do if you didn't go back?' she asked him.

'How do you mean?'

'Yeah, where would you go? Where is your "wonderland"?'

In reality, now that he thought about it, Orestes had never imagined not going back. He had imagined going back, but to a life that wasn't his. It was similar, but it was not the same. He lived in the same house, but he didn't have a wife, or a dead daughter, or a living one. He kept tropical fish in the living room and lots of books in his study: very respectable books, written by him, and he was no longer called Orestes. *Nobody called Orestes writes respectable books.*

He looked out of the window at the sky: it was covered with clouds. The threat of rain had been hanging in the air for days, but it was not raining. Beyond the road, there was a hill and the ruins of a castle. Yara yawned, said something about a project she was working on and mentioned the expression "digital inclusion". Orestes nodded. He thought her hair was looking slightly droopier. A while ago, the curls had been tighter.

'We still don't know what the priorities are, the world grew too fast and the Millennium Goals are a joke,' Yara was saying.

Orestes used to think that the reason his head had grown empty of ideas had something to do with his family. Now he saw Yara and thought the same thing again: people who had no family could devote themselves more to ideas and less to people. Emotional proximity to certain people, to children, for example – knowing what was going on with them, whether it was good or bad, or dull or intense – took up a lot of space in one's mind. And the important ideas ended up being pushed out.

'...the organisations are as inefficient as the govern-ments.' Her mop of hair continued to deflate. Yara was clearly one of those women who, as a feminist, flaunted how little she cared about her appearance. She would not denigrate herself by running a comb through her hair, she would never relax her tangled mop to make it tamer, more pleasing to the male gaze. Or perhaps, Yara did the opposite: every morning she knotted it all up using one of those lice combs, so that nobody would accuse her of having combed her hair. Orestes wondered if Becky was a feminist.

'…don't you think, Orestes?' Yara brought a spoonful of food to her mouth and chewed. Her eyes were open very wide, looking at him. He nodded.

★

After the restaurant they went to an old music hall, with the face of Lucio Battisti plastered all over the walls. Yara propped her elbows on the table, leaning forward slightly, her cleavage revealing heavy-hanging breasts. She was not wearing a bra.

'I lost them both,' said Orestes, self-absorbed.

'What did you say?' said Yara.

'There's not even a word to describe my situation,' he went on. 'Children without parents are orphans, but parents without children, what are they? Bad parents?'

Yara shook her head doubtfully. She didn't seem interested anymore. Orestes drank his wine and stopped talking.

'And how was the conference?' said Yara.

'Awful.'

'Why?'

He took another sip of wine and his chest hurt.

'Really bad, everything was so mediocre.'

'I heard there was an interesting lecture.'

'Oh yeah?'

'A friend of mine went.'

Orestes sipped his wine, savouring it.

Yara was talking about some school of thought or other based on using the marketing concept of "bisociation" to deal with the most pressing educational issues. Orestes shook his head. 'Those concepts are just a distraction; the ideas are there, they've always been there, and we must use them.' Orestes had not attended the lecture, so he didn't have much else to say.

Orestes had not attended any lectures.

'No, darling, I think that the ideas ran out a while ago.'

They probably wouldn't give him the attendance certificate. A few days ago, he had talked to one of the organisers, an abrasive woman in her twenties. 'A minimum level of attendance is required to issue the certificates, sir.'

'But I am more qualified than the actual lecturers.'

The girl raised an eyebrow dismissively. 'I'll see what I can do.'

Yara poured herself more wine.

Orestes felt a wave of intense heat, and suddenly wanted to take off his clothes.

He had a disgusting body: a showcase of loose, sagging skin. He had not looked at his body naked in a mirror for a long time, because he now slept in Rosa's old room, and there was no mirror in there. There had been one until Becky took it away.

'"…new approaches to old issues",' Yara was saying, in English.

There was no mirror in Rosa's bathroom either. There was a window, through which you could see a rooftop, a sliver of sky, mould, lizards. You could also see tree branches. Before he got into the shower, Orestes looked at his reflection in the window, superimposed over the green of the branches. He liked looking at himself from all angles. It was not a clear reflection of him, but almost: the white hair forming a halo on his head, his face blurred, his chest sunken, his tummy and backside flabby, his cock hanging flaccidly over his balls. Orestes barely had balls anymore: they had been crushed, consumed. When he went back to his bedroom after showering, he could feel the water dripping off them under his robe and thought, they're empty sacks, an old woman's sunken cheeks.

'Talk to her about something, Orestes, make up a story

that involves both of you.'

Orestes looked at Yara, puzzled.

'Talk to who?'

Yara shook her head with some annoyance, put her hands on the table and stood up. Her top revealed even more cleavage: Orestes could see the beginnings of a nipple, an enormous areola.

'To Becky!' she replied.

★

The following morning, Orestes did not take a shower.

He had not showered for some time.

He only showered when he started to smell strongly, and people at the university began looking at him oddly. He rarely smelled his own scent, what he did notice was a change in the texture of his skin: a shiny layer that he worried would become a layer of dirt that was impossible to wash off. Then he set about scrubbing himself with a loofah, turning his skin red.

The previous night, he'd got in after midnight, with a stomach ache. He vomited up bile because he hadn't eaten anything. He turned on the TV and watched a documentary about a tribe in Indonesia in which the women ate their placenta after giving birth. By the time it finished, it was almost daylight and he couldn't get to sleep.

He then went out into the hallway where there was a computer connected to the internet. He had not heard anything from home in days; he had tried to call, but there was no answer. He had only spoken once to the nurse, who answered all his questions dismissively. He had two new messages on his voicemail. One from a student asking about his grade, and another from the dean of the faculty asking how the conference went and saying that they had a frame ready and waiting for his 'honourable certificate'. Then he asked Orestes to bring him some cigars they sold in duty free at Rome airport. There were a lot of instructions, and they were numbered: 1. Squeeze it gently between thumb and forefinger to test its condition: it should be firm, but not hard. 2. The colour should be uniform throughout the whole cigar, and the leaves must have a certain shine…

The hot feeling came back. He had a hazy image of his daughter's face smashed against the ground. But it was not Rosa's, it was Becky's.

He went back to his room and dialled her number.

'Becky?'

'Yes.'

'How are you?'

'Going out, I came back in to answer the phone. Right now, I can't…'

'I just thought perhaps you'd like me to send you my itinerary.'

'No, what for? I can't come and meet you, I told you, I'm going to be out.'

'Darling, I want to tell you a story about when you were a little girl.'

'Dad, please.'

'Perhaps you don't remember, and if you ask your mum about it she'll deny it, just to punish me…'

Becky sighed.

'Your poor mother. But she wasn't always like that. What happened was, when she had both of you, she expelled all of the good she had inside her, and was left with just the remains of that disgusting placenta… Did you know that some females eat it after giving birth?'

'Okay, well I really have to go.'

'Wait, please.'

'But…'

'Two minutes, darling.'

'I've got people waiting for me.'

'I want to tell you about a conversation we had when you were really little.'

'Are you drunk?'

'You can't have been more than three when I told you who Manuel Sotomayor was, your great-grandfather, and you looked at me as if you knew. We were alone in your room, you'd been crying, yelling and stamping your feet. And I didn't understand what was the matter with you and didn't know any of the songs your mum used to sing to you, so I picked you up and told you about my grand-father, that is, your great-grandfather. I talked to you for a long time because I didn't know what else to do, and you made those strange noises that babies make when they seem to be content. What I remember most is your eyes, which were fixed on my mouth, without blinking. You had these enormous eyes that filled your whole face.'

Becky said nothing. He could not even hear her breathing. Orestes began to think she had hung up, but he didn't care.

'…that day you made me feel like there was nothing in the world you were more interested in than that badly-told story. And I thought: I have the power to fill her little empty head with ideas that someday she's going to transform into something else, into something better than what I'm telling her, into something better than the original story and something better than me.' He stopped talking. He let out a deep and – he thought – clumsy sob. Like a drill through concrete. This story was true. It had actually been Rosa, not Becky, but nobody was going to know.

'Becky?' He was still crying.

'What?' she replied.

They were silent for a moment, as Orestes' breathing

gradually returned to normal. Then she spoke again: 'Send me your itinerary again.' And she hung up.

FISH SOUP

Very early one morning, as Mr Aldo Villafora was sleeping, he was disturbed by the pungent smell of boiled fish. It was not yet the smell of soup, it still needed seasoning and herbs, and, of course, the aniseed that Helena added to everything. Or it was the smell of soup, but an insipid, watery soup. He thought he must be dreaming. After tossing and turning in bed for a while, even covering his head with the pillow, Villafora finally got up. He sat up and took a couple of deep breaths. The foul odour entered his nostrils, went down his gullet and settled in his stomach. It was like when dead fish washed up on the beach and nobody picked them up for weeks. They just lay there rotting, and the air would be filled with the stink of blackened, dead flesh.

The sand in the hourglass on the bedside table was still almost all at the top, with only a meagre pile at the bottom. It was the start of another hour: Villafora could not remember when the last one had finished, when he had turned the hourglass over. But he was not surprised by this. Lately he hardly noticed when night became day.

He got out of bed and wrapped the sheet around his waist. The mirror on the wall reflected the image of a man worn out by working late nights: thin and saggy, his skin transparent like tracing paper, with blue veins snaking all over his body like a hydrographic map of a country with an abundance of rivers. Villafora was the owner of an old bar, which was also his home. The bar was named "Helena" after his wife, who had died from a long and painful disease that took hold of every bone in her body and left her prostrate in bed, delirious. The bar was on the ground floor: it was a spartan place, an industrial drinking hole with wooden tables and chairs, and a large bar with high stools. It had floor-to-ceiling windows looking out onto a side street – in the morning this alleyway was filled with grocery stalls and at night, with prostitutes who, for lack of clients, often came to hang out in the bar. The house was on the upper floor. It consisted of a small living room with a window, and an adjoining bedroom and bathroom. Through the living room window there was a view of the harbour, which was not much of a harbour. It was more of a dumping ground for clapped-out old fishing boats. The city was a tourist resort, the kind of place backpackers and young runaway couples passed through.

Helena's death had changed the way the bar was run: for example, lately they only served fried sardines. When Helena was alive, however, she persuaded the market stall owners to keep the leftover fish heads for her and every evening she made soup. The soup was popular in the early morning, when the drunks started to feel hungry and all she had to do was warm it up. But as soon as Helena died, Villafora decided that food would be the lowest priority in that place: if he was eating meagre, insipid meals, why should he slave away to fill other people's bellies?

So, on that morning which smelled of fish, Mr Aldo Villafora got out of bed, wrapped the sheet around his waist, checked that he looked the same as he always did in the mirror on the wall, and got ready to go downstairs. He was outraged to think that Wally, the barman, or Grace, the cleaning lady, might be making fish soup. Because that meant they were going against his orders, ignoring his wishes. So, that fish swimming in the cooking pot, how did it get there, then? Villafora imagined himself scolding them, and them just insolently shrugging their shoulders at him. Oh, maybe it came leaping up from the harbour all by itself and dived into the boiling water, like some kind of kamikaze fish, maybe that's it? But when Villafora reached the kitchen, neither Wally nor Grace were making soup. Then he remembered that they weren't even there: they had gone to a bar down by the harbour to watch the final of the Super Bowl. A local talent nicknamed Chichi Pimiento was playing.

'Who's there?' said Villafora in a firm voice. Nobody answered. He straightened himself up and walked around the kitchen, his chest puffed out, shoulders pulled back. 'Who's th-'

But he didn't finish his sentence, because suddenly he heard the pathetic mewing of Penelope, that cat that Wally had given Helena. He had brought the little scruff ball in off the street one day, saying 'I've brought you a present, Doña Helena.' Villafora saw that as an affront. 'Nobody gives my wife presents apart from me.' But as soon as Helena saw the cat, she fell in love with it. Penelope meowed again and Villafora realised where she was. He ran to the oven, opened it and took out the cat, who was exhausted and caked in old grease. The oven was turned off, but it was one of those industrial machines that shuts like a vacuum seal when the door is closed. He poured some milk out into a little dish and carried Penelope into the bar. He set her down on the floor and sat behind the counter, propped his elbows on the bar and looked at the empty room: the chairs stacked up on the tables, the filthy floor, the mildewed walls hung with pictures of places he would never go – Paris, New York, Tokyo, London, Granada. Helena had put those pictures up; she was a big fan of *Travel and Living*.

Villafora yawned. He remembered the fish smell that had woken him and realised that it had gone. He whirled round to look at the box containing Helena's ashes, on the top shelf of the spirits and liquors, as if accusing her of waking him up with that lousy smell. But he immediately banished the idea from his mind, because Mr Aldo Villafora was not a mystical or fanciful person, or a schizophrenic. He wasn't even a Christian. To him, Helena's ashes were just that: ashes. And, although he sometimes looked at them nostalgically, he knew very well that at some point he would have to do something with them, but he still wasn't sure what. Scattering them into the sea seemed too sappy but flushing them down the toilet was no solution either.

★

Villafora opened his eyes. He had fallen asleep. The cat was no longer there. In the bar, however, a man and woman were going at it against a wall, slobbering over one another like a pair of dogs. Villafora hated those kinds of displays in the bar, particularly so early in the day. He glanced over to check that the main door to the bar was closed. They must have come in through the window. Perhaps they were robbers.

He grabbed a knife from underneath the counter and walked slowly towards them. In a swift movement, the man hurled the woman down onto a table and wrenched up her skirt. He yanked down his trousers and pulled out an enormous member, the most impressive thing Villafora had ever seen.

'Hey!' he cried, and the guy turned to look at him.

It was Tellez, the sailor: he savagely penetrated the woman while she let out hoarse cries. Villafora launched himself at Tellez, shoving him as hard as he could. Tellez barely moved, but just enough for Villafora to see the woman's face.

'Helena?'

Helena ignored him. She was lost in an expression of pleasure that Villafora had never seen her make. Her legs were splayed wide; she was impaled by Tellez' huge member. Villafora ran to the other side of the table, grabbed a handful of Helena's hair, pulled her head back and slit her throat.

'Whore.'

★

'Señor Villafora?' It was Grace.

Villafora opened his eyes and saw the girl looking awkwardly to one side, as if she had a cricked neck. Then he realised that he was naked: the sheet had fallen to the floor.

'Sorry, Grace.' He picked up the sheet and tied it around his waist again. 'I fell asleep there because somebody left the cat in the oven, and because of the terrible smell of fish that...'

Grace stared at him as if he were a madman.

'What's wrong?' said Villafora, and the girl walked off into the kitchen without saying anything. Villafora thought that she was just bad-mannered; but after a few seconds, as he was about to go back to bed, Grace came out of the kitchen, this time with Wally, and the two of them stood there gawping at him. Wally's face was contorted, his eyes red. Villafora thought perhaps it was because he'd been boozing the night away in honour of Chichi Pimiento.

'She's dead,' said Wally.

Grace started to cry and Villafora looked at them blankly.

'Huh?' he said. 'What's wrong with you, have you both gone loopy?' He held the knot in the sheet with one hand and with the other, he pointed at them, threateningly. 'One

119

of you has done something terrible – you don't do that to an animal.'

Grace cried even harder. Wally hugged Penelope, who now lay limply in his arms. How had the cat got there? Villafora felt tired. He squeezed his eyes shut then opened them again.

'What happened to Penelope?' he asked, confused.

'You killed her,' said Wally, his eyes filled with rage.

'Me?' Villafora could not stand the tiredness, his knees were trembling, he could hardly stand. 'Give her some milk, that'll make her better.' And he turned and started to climb the stairs. 'Then, take her out of there, put her in the street and…'. The words faded to a sigh.

*

The bed was damp. Villafora fell in and out of a fitful sleep, unable to get comfortable. Every time he breathed he heard a whistling sound and his chest hurt. The hourglass on the bedside table still had almost all its sand in the upper bulb and, in the lower one, a mound barely higher than it had been in the morning. He could smell fish again. And he could hear whispering.

As he lay there dozing, Mr Aldo Villafora dreamed that he was on a ship to Europe, dressed in a waistcoat with gold buttons. Helena was with him, and so was Penelope, who had a collar round her neck and looked like one of those little porcelain cats they sold at fairs. The sun was shining, but it was not too hot, so they were sitting on the prow of the boat looking out to sea. He was sitting in a comfortable deckchair, and Helena was standing, staring out at the horizon. She wore a hat with a ribbon trim, and a dress nipped in at the waist with a long, full skirt. Now that he thought about it, the two of them were dressed in a strangely old-fashioned way. Penelope was sitting on another chair, watching him. Every now and then he would make little gestures and faces at her. He was fond of that cat, although he didn't like to admit it. For Mr Aldo Villafora, a love of animals was typical of people who lacked character.

He could hear piano music coming from somewhere, and Villafora closed his eyes, breathed in the salt on the breeze and felt contented, relaxed. Villafora and his wife had never had a holiday.

'Helena, doesn't that sound like that song, the one about a boat carrying a cross of... of what?' he asked.

She turned slowly to face him with a vacant expression.

'I don't know, darling.'

'Is something wrong?'

'No.'

But something clearly was. Helena looked back out to sea and Villafora followed her gaze. There was a small boat, being rowed by a sailor. The sailor was also looking at Helena, saying something to her that Villafora could not quite make out.

'Who is that, Helena?' he asked.

'Who?'

She carried on looking at the man, smiling with her head tilted. Then Villafora saw that it was Rodríguez, the sailor, with his caveman demeanour, rapidly approaching their ship.

'Come here, Helena. Come and sit with me.'

'I can't.'

'Why not?'

Helena shrugged. Villafora looked for Penelope in the other chair, but she was no longer there. Now there was just a basin containing a pile of fish, flapping around in their death throes. The smell was overpowering.

'I've had enough; all this fish is making me sick...'

Villafora covered his nose.

Helena walked quickly over and sat down next to him. Her dress clung tightly to her torso, her heaving breasts bulging out of it, like the whores in the alley.

'You must eat the soup, darling,' Helena said to him, with a bowl and spoon in her hand. She stirred and blew on the clear liquid. It gave off the same vile-smelling steam that had disturbed his sleep that morning.

Villafora shook his head.

'I don't want soup, I really don't.'

'It's good for your brain, it's good for your joints. The doctor said…'

'Which doctor?'

'The fat doctor, darling.'

He looked around to confirm that they were alone in the middle of the sea, but when he tried to tell Helena, she had vanished.

*

When Mr Aldo Villafora opened his eyes again, it was almost night. The door to his room was open and through it he could see the living room window that overlooked the harbour. In the sky there were a few scattered stars, and a sliver of a moon. On the bedside table, the hourglass was still not empty.

'Bloody thing,' said Villafora. His mouth felt dry.

How was it possible for an hourglass to stop working? He sat up in bed, with difficulty. He was finding it increasingly hard to get up, he was getting thinner and weaker. From there, he looked at himself in the mirror on the wall and thought how haggard he looked. He reached out to grab the hourglass, but instead he found a revolver in his hand. He looked at it, then tucked it under the pillow, where he used to keep it for safety.

He was still tired. Soon he would have to go down to the bar. Wally must have opened up by now, and Grace was not good at handling the cash register. She was too easily distracted by the customers, who would strike up conversations, knowing she would get confused and undercharge them. At that time of day, it wasn't too serious, but when the sailors started coming in from the harbour, at around eight o'clock, everything would get complicated. They came in hungry, already half-cut, and in the bar, they seemed to completely forget themselves. They would grab sardines in handfuls, shovelling them into their mouths like animals. Sometimes they would rub them in the face of a distracted companion and wipe their hands on their clothes; the stink became unbearable. There wasn't a single night that Grace did not have to clean up vomit. When there were whores in the bar, the sailors smeared food all over their tits and ate off them; the women's shrieks upset Grace even more, and she often ended up fleeing in tears, leaving the cash register unattended. Villafora knew all of this because he had once been ill for a couple of weeks and asked Grace to fill in for him on the cash register. But by the third day, the girl was such a nervous wreck that Helena had to leave her post in the kitchen to cover for her. His wife had stoically endured all those nights; when she got into bed at dawn, she was swollen with exhaustion, and Villafora broke down in sobs and apologies. But she would tell him not to worry, that they were going to save enough money, close the bar and go on a trip; then everything would become just a bad memory.

'A bad memory, my love.' He felt like he could hear her voice.

Villafora tried to stand up, but something was stopping him. A weight on his shoulders, a terrible pain in his temples. He squeezed his eyes shut. He could hear shouting from downstairs. A fight must have broken out. He mustered some strength and managed to stand up, went out of the bedroom and leaned over the inner balcony overlooking the bar. A ring of customers had formed around a pair of sailors who were hurling punches at one another. A woman was trying to separate them.

'Grace?' Villafora called out.

But there was so much noise, and his voice was so feeble, that nobody heard him. He started making his way slowly down the stairs; every step he took caused his whole body to ache. At some point, as he descended the stairs, the fight stopped looking like a fight: Tellez and Rodriguez were laughing and passing the woman between them; she fell into their arms, one after the other. When Villafora reached the bottom step, he saw Rodriguez open his fly and sit down on a chair. The woman hitched up her skirt, sat down on him, face-to-face, and let herself fall backwards into the arms of Tellez, who held her while she writhed: it was Helena. Her blouse was half off, revealing her bra. She had lipstick on. She was laughing, enjoying it and laughing. Villafora stood next to them and stayed there for a few seconds; he felt like he was hovering above the floor, watching everything as if it were a film, or a memory. He pressed the tip of the revolver against Helena's forehead and pulled the trigger.

★

The bang startled him. Villafora put his hand to his chest, sat up and saw an explosion of fireworks out of the living room window. In the background, shouts could be heard, and downstairs the music had been turned up so high that it made his head pound. He lay down again. In fact, he felt as if someone was gently pushing him by the shoulders.

'Grace, ask them to turn the volume down, please, a little respect…'

Villafora heard the voice of his wife from far away, as if from inside a deep cavern. He half opened his eyes and saw a tearful Grace standing in the doorway to the bedroom. She turned and left. In the living room, with his back to Villafora, a fat man was looking out of the window at the fireworks.

'Who is…?' Villafora tried to say.

'Sshh, don't strain yourself,' said Helena, who was sitting on a stool next to his bed.

The fat man turned and walked towards the bedroom.

'Chichi Pimiento's team won. Good lord, if they go on like this, they'll have to declare a curfew.'

Helena rearranged Villafora's pillow, pulled the sheet up to his chest.

'How's he doing?' said the fat man.

Helena shook her head.

'He's saying strange things, he's complaining about a smell, but I can't smell anything.'

Helena tidied the things on the bedside table: a bowl of watery soup, a bottle of pills, syringes. The fat man laid a hand on her shoulder and said, 'Don't worry, this stage is compl–'

'Will he know what's happening?' she cut him off, her voice hoarse.

The fat man sighed.

Grace came back into the room, with Wally, his face burning, eyes bloodshot.

'Well?' he said, looking around anxiously.

'What happened to Penelope?' said Villafora.

'Sshh,' Helena repeated, dabbing his forehead with a handkerchief.

'Who?' said Wally.

Helena shrugged. 'A little cat we had years ago, who…'
She was interrupted mid-sentence by the noise of a
firecracker. Helena looked at the bedside table again and
turned over the hourglass, which was empty at last. She
sighed and took hold of Villafora's hand.

'What now?' Grace stammered, looking at the fat man,
who was leaning against the wall with such composure that
Villafora found it offensive.

The fat man took a deep breath and replied, 'Now, we
wait.'

Something We Never Were

When Salvador asked Eileen to be his girlfriend, she said no. She was having none of that boyfriend and girlfriend crap; what she was interested in was questioning certain paradigms. And seeing as all Salvador wanted to do was sleep with her, he decided not to contradict her.

Eileen was tiny and skinny, red-haired and, so she said, part Irish. Salvador was too tall, and he didn't like it, so he would stoop slightly when he walked. The night they started dating, Eileen took Salvador to her apartment to watch an inspirational film. It was already the early hours of the morning and he thought she might put on a porn film, but she put on *The Third Man*. Every now and then, Eileen's dad would poke his head around the door of the room where they were watching TV. He was wearing long pyjamas, cup of tea in hand. 'Great film,' he said.

The sex would happen in the apartment Salvador shared with his friend Matías.

Eileen's first request was for him to read out loud while she sucked him off.

'I won't be able to concentrate on both things,' he told her, and Eileen replied that the only thing he had to concentrate on was the reading, she would take care of the other thing. And that's what they used to do: he read out loud and she did her part. Salvador read poetry or extracts of novels, which Eileen chose; or he read long essays that Eileen had written at university and that, at first, gave him nothing but headaches. He couldn't get it up in the beginning, and it was frustrating. But Eileen persisted so tenaciously that he ended up getting used to it, and even came to enjoy it.

Three months into their relationship Eileen started taking money from his bedside table. The amount was different every time, and she moved the money from the table to her purse as naturally as if she were opening the fridge for a bottle of water. Salvador didn't say anything. He didn't know what to say; it didn't seem fair to him, he wasn't exactly rolling in money. One day, as they were strolling through a plaza together – she was talking about some island in the Pacific which was sinking, and she was concerned because they were going to have to relocate all its inhabitants to different cities around the world, where they would no doubt be rejected – Salvador asked her:

'Are you charging me for sex?'

Eileen burst out laughing. She grabbed his hand and steered him towards a bench, where they sat down.

'If you and I were something different to what we are, the fact that I took money off your bedside table might mean that we are engaging in a commercial transaction. But with us, it doesn't work like that, right?'

Salvador shook his head, although he wasn't completely sure he understood.

'The rules are different for us, Salvador.'

'Right.'

'The money's there on the bedside table, like food in a shop, or books in a library, and I am happy in the knowledge that, at least in our limited personal space, relationships are governed by the principles of common decency that you and I share.'

'Uh-huh.'

'Anyway, it's not like I take everything that's on the

bedside table, I take strictly what I need, like you take what you need from me.' She smiled, stood up from the bench and resumed her spiel about the sinking island.

★

'Why don't you just give it any old ending and be done with it?' asked Salvador.

Eileen was writing a script for a play that she just couldn't seem to finish. She had spent months contemplating the ending. She was snappy, anxious and had begun chain-smoking. They barely had any sex.

'Sweetheart?' said Salvador.

Eileen had sunk into a rare silence, her face contorted.

'Leave me alone, I'm thinking.'

She was naked, lying on the bed on her back: Eileen had such small tits that when she lay down they disappeared. Salvador was leaning against the bedstead. The sheets felt damp with sweat, the sweltering air seemed to cling to them.

'But if you write more, nobody will read it, nobody reads things that long.'

'I read much longer things.'

Eileen jumped up and left the room. Her slender body was as agile as a rabbit. She no longer had red hair, nor Irish descent; she had died her hair jet black and now she looked just like any other girl at university. When she turned up with black hair, Salvador was a little disappointed: her red hair was the thing he liked best about her. That, and her mouth, which was huge and looked slightly out of proportion to her face. And the sex, of course. Eileen was the best sex he'd ever had.

Salvador pulled on a pair of shorts and went to look for her. She had to be in the living room. Matías had moved out a month ago because Eileen was spending too much time in the apartment and he couldn't stand her. 'It's her or me,' he'd said. Salvador shrugged and looked down at the floor. That's when he knew he was in love.

He found her at the kitchen table, rolling one of her cigarettes that dropped strands of tobacco everywhere. They ended up in everything: food, water, coffee.

'I think it's going to be a silent play,' said Eileen.

'Silent?'

'Yes, nobody will say anything, maybe there won't even be any actors, it will be an empty stage, a blank script.'

Salvador sighed. He missed Matías. It was Saturday, they could have been drinking beer, playing cards, in silence. Eileen lit her cigarette and walked towards the balcony. He followed her but stopped in the doorway. The view outside was of an empty lot, and beyond that, a grey wall. Next to theirs was another balcony, with a guy sitting on it, drinking beer.

'Hi Eileen,' said the guy.

'Hi Ricardo.'

Eileen was still naked.

During the time he had been living there, Salvador had never interacted with any of the neighbours. He had passed some of them on the stairs; he had once rung the bell of the apartment below to ask them to turn down the music: they never opened the door. So, he had no idea who Ricardo was, or anybody else. Eileen knew exactly who was who.

★

Eileen considered ejaculation a very private thing, and something that should not be wasted, that's what she told him. She suggested that from then on, he should wait until she'd gone, and then jerk off.

130

'But I like it better when you're here, because…'

'Sshh—' she put a finger to his lips. 'You have to learn, Salvador.'

But why did she say that? Salvador didn't understand: a short while ago she had arrived, babbling, talking about how her script was progressing. 'I'll be the next David Mamet.' She pulled her dress over her head and threw it on the floor. She had no underwear on. She tied up her hair with a band she had round her wrist. She jumped into bed, where Salvador was reading some photocopies and told him to watch her do it: she went down between his legs and sucked him off like she'd never done before, and he didn't even have to recite anything.

That's why Salvador was surprised when she said what she said. Then, just like that, she got up off the bed and carried on talking about her script. Salvador didn't move. He followed the sound of her movements around the apartment. They were minimal sounds. The fabric of the dress sliding over her skin; one wooden sandal stepping on the floor, then the other one, both sandals, *clack clack clack*, the fridge door opening; a swig of water or maybe Coke, which she glugged down; and *clack clack clack*, the notes sliding off the bedside table into her purse; the bony hands smoothing down her dress; the keys.

'Bye, my love.'

Salvador raised his hand, feeling weak.

'Bye.'

★

Eileen became notorious at the university and gave a talk about her play. A journalism student asked her if her script was fatalistic.

'Why do you say that?'

'Because they all die.'

'That's a very simplistic view.'

Salvador was in the audience, feeling awkward. Everyone was talking about how wonderful Eileen's work was, when in reality there was no work: a group of actors came onstage, collapsed on top of one another and the curtain came down. Then it opened again, and they did exactly the same thing, and so on, several times. Nobody ever said anything.

'...what I mean to say...' the journalism student continued with his lengthy question, 'is that the fact that civilization repeats itself throughout the course of history, reiterating its successes and failures, in a vicious cycle, is a way of condemning humanity to the idea of an unambiguous fate, which will lead people to the same tragic result, over and over again...'

Perhaps he was a philosophy student, thought Salvador, and shifted in his chair. He was uncomfortable, twisted.

'Could you be more precise?' Eileen said to him, crossing and uncrossing her legs, looking at the student as if she wanted to jump on top of him and lick his face.

'Sure, my question is whether your script postulates that nobody can be saved from their fate, and that this fate is, and always will be, the same tragic fate.'

There was a murmur of approval. Salvador coughed and looked at his watch. The conference had started an hour and a half ago. He was hungry. Eileen replied:

'My script doesn't postulate anything, but if it did, then perhaps it would postulate something that Nietzsche hadn't already postulated.'

There was laughter in the audience, guffaws. People choking on their laughter, having to be patted on the back. Salvador didn't understand anything: he gripped the arms of his chair, his jaw clenched. The student took a bow, raised his arms then let them drop in a gesture of defeat. He shook his head several times and sat down.

When the talk was over, they went to the cafeteria, but everyone was crowding around Eileen, and Salvador had to move away. He ordered a soda and two empanadas and looked at her from a corner: Eileen was wearing a dress he had given her. It was blue, like her newly dyed hair. Salvador wolfed down the empanadas in two bites and ordered another. From the table where she was sitting with her fans, Eileen looked over at him every now and then and waved. She was going to leave him, it was obvious. He finished his third empanada, wiped his hands on his jeans and was on his way out, when he heard Eileen's voice.

'Wait for me.' She ran over, jumped up on him and flung her arms round his neck. 'Get me out of here. Let's go for a drink.'

They went to a bar. The weather was good, so they sat outside on the terrace. Eileen was in a good mood, and slightly tipsy: she was on her fourth beer.

'So, what about that question this afternoon?' said Salvador.

'Which question?'

'That guy… he was an idiot, right?'

'You think?'

Salvador shrugged. He downed his beer and asked the waiter for a cigarette.

'My answer was idiotic,' said Eileen, 'not his question.'

'But everyone loved your answer, they laughed, they applauded you.'

'Nobody got it. They laughed because they thought it was a joke: it wasn't a joke, but I said it in a way that seemed like it was. And people often get things wrong.'

'Mm–hm.'

Salvador wondered why the hell you would make a

joke that wasn't a joke. He finished his beer but didn't order another one because he was almost out of money and he knew that Eileen wouldn't offer to chip in. He wanted to go home. He wanted Eileen to take off that hideous dress. For the first time, he felt like breaking up with her, but he didn't know how to do it. It would be better if she did it.

'Are you pissed off?'

Salvador shrugged.

'Do you want me to explain what Nietzsche said?'

'Not really.'

'It's nothing special, I don't even know why that guy mentioned it, it's hardly related to my script.'

Salvador rubbed his neck.

'...and it's not Nietzsche's idea anyway, he got it from the Stoics.'

'Mm-hm.'

'Anyway, what he proposes is a repetition of the world, i.e. that the world ends and then rebuilds itself so that the same acts occur again, without any possibility of variation.'

'That's absurd.'

'No, it's a cycle. Simple. It's like saying day and night, the moon and the sun, the seasons...' Now she seemed irritated.

'Mm-hm.'

Eileen drank her beer, blinked slowly, then took his hand.

'And Nietzsche said that it's not only acts that recur, but feelings too.' He had heartburn, it must have been the beer. Or the cigarette. 'In other words, if the world ended today, tomorrow you and I would fall in love again.'

Salvador wanted to burp, but he held it in.

★

Eileen was snuggled up in one of Salvador's hoodies, which looked like a sleeping bag on her. She was cold. Salvador wasn't, but he closed the balcony door so that she would be more comfortable. Then he set about preparing an onion soup.

'I haven't seen Ricardo for days,' said Eileen, who was lying on the living room sofa.

'Who?' Salvador added pieces of toasted bread to the soup.

'Ricardo, the neighbour.'

'Maybe he's dead,' said Salvador, and laughed. Eileen didn't join in.

Matías would have laughed.

He served up two bowls of soup and carried them into the dining room. They ate, and afterwards, Eileen put her head down on the table, sighed heavily and closed her eyes. Salvador took the empty dishes back into the kitchen.

'How much time has passed?' said Eileen.

He turned to look at her.

'Since when?'

'Since I fell asleep.'

'When did you fall asleep?'

Salvador returned to the table with an apple and a knife.

'I wonder what happens to people when they spend too much time together,' said Eileen, staring at him.

Salvador shrugged and grimaced. 'Um.'

'They disappoint each other,' said Eileen. 'As you get to know someone, disappointment is inevitable.'

'You reckon?' Salvador was peeling the apple; he didn't like the skin.

'There are ways of pretending to be blind, but one day you'll have to face up to reality, and reality is always disappointing.'

Salvador popped a piece of apple into his mouth and said, 'And which day might that be?'

'I don't know, it's different for everyone, I suppose in your case it will be the day you wake up with me by your side and wonder how that shrivelled old bean got there.'

Salvador laughed. Eileen didn't.

'...and even if your own body deteriorates rapidly, and you end being a flabby, smelly old ape, which will certainly happen to you one day, the other body will always seem worse to you, because repulsion towards your own body is always more bearable than towards someone else's.'

Salvador wasn't laughing anymore: he had grown bored. And a piece of apple had got lodged in his throat. He swallowed, and it went down, but it still hurt. He thumped his chest a couple of times, to help it move down his throat.

'I'll never be disappointed by you,' he said afterwards. He thought that would resolve the issue.

'Of course you will,' said Eileen, 'and vice versa.' She got up from the table, said she was going for a cigarette. Salvador carried on eating his apple, thinking that yes, now she was going to leave him. There was no going back. It was better that way; Eileen was weird, Matías was right.

'...insignificant people take longer to get disappointed because they are motivated by hope.' Eileen was smoking. Her dishevelled blue hair looked like candy floss. 'They spend a good part of their mediocre lives hoping that at some point, something amazing is going to happen to them, something that will change their life. But in the end, they're all disappointed.'

She was worked up, talking at a volume that Salvador would have liked to moderate with a blow to the head. He finished off the last piece of apple, chewing very slowly, counting each bite, focusing on the sound his teeth made.

Then Eileen sat on his lap, wrapping her arms around his neck.

'In the end, we all disappoint each other. All of us, the

more we get to know each other.' She kissed him.

And he felt relieved.

★

'I don't get it, Salvador, we had an agreement and it was pretty convenient, especially for you. I don't think it's fair or right or decent, but most of all I don't think it's logical for you to say you don't want to see me anymore. You don't even have a reason. You don't have one, do you?'

Salvador did not reply, he knew by now that when Eileen asked those kind of questions, they were never actually meant for him. They were on the pavement outside the front door of the building. It was cold out. He had drunk several rums to pluck up the courage to say what he had said to her.

'What reason could you possibly have?' Eileen was pacing up and down, and he was watching her from the front step. 'If the agreement consisted of our relationship being built on the basis that there was no relationship, so that neither of us could impose the characteristics of the connection on the other…'

'What connection?'

'That was clear, wasn't it?'

'What?'

If Matías had been there, he could have asked him if he understood. Perhaps he, looking at it as an outsider, might have understood. It seemed like centuries since he had last seen Matías.

'The thing is, if we could only put this case to someone neutral, but trustworthy…'

'That's what I was…' Salvador tried to say.

'Someone like, like who?' Eileen stopped, put her hands on her hips and looked at the ground.

'Like Matías.'

'Like Mikhail Bakunin, for example.' Eileen started pacing again. 'The man would choose to dismiss the case for being riddled with elementary errors. And the thing is, Salvador,' she turned to look at him, 'your problem is discursive: you always get stuck on the first proposition. For example, you say, "I don't want to carry on with this", but then you never put forward a convincing argument. Then we can't talk, or discuss, let alone put an end to "this thing" that doesn't exist.' She came closer, stood with her arms folded in front of him. 'You can't expect us to stop being something we never were.'

Salvador got up from the step, moved forward and took her by the shoulders. He held her shining gaze, looked at her half-open mouth and sighed deeply.

'Eileen,' he said, 'I don't understand you.'

'What don't you understand?'

'Anything you say.'

Eileen pulled away from him.

'You don't understand that the destruction of the non-condition is equivalent to the condition?!' she roared.

Salvador tried to hold her, to calm her down, but she dodged his grip. Salvador wanted to grab her by the neck and smash her face repeatedly into the pavement.

'I need you to explain to me,' said Eileen, out of breath. Rivulets of smudged black makeup were running down her face. When had she cried? 'Explain to me,' she insisted.

Salvador's head was pounding. He clenched his fists and inhaled the freezing night air, like ammonia in his nostrils. He wondered what they were doing outside in that weather. He took another breath and felt a sharp twinge between his eyebrows.

'It's cold,' he said.

Eileen slapped him. He didn't even see it coming.

For such a tiny hand, the blow was hard and painful, but the icy air numbed it instantly. Salvador turned and went into the building. Through the glass door he could see Eileen's minute body: her strange little blue head shaking in confusion, as if trying to escape the thick cloud that hovered above her.

SKY AND POPLARS

Airports made her nervous, but it was not because of goodbyes. She did not have a single memory of saying goodbye to someone before a flight. What she didn't like was the waiting, the uncomfortable seats, the pervasive smell of the toilets. And the people travelling, she hated them more than anything. Nor had she taken all that many flights. As a little girl she had never travelled by plane because her parents had no money, and now as an adult, she did not see the appeal. Perhaps it was an acquired taste, she thought, like eating blue cheese.

'Have a good trip.' Jerónimo handed over her suitcase, wrapped in fluorescent plastic.

Emanuella got up from the seat where she had been waiting. One of her legs had gone to sleep. The last few months had left her very overweight and her circulation was poor. Jerónimo had insisted on paying extra to have her suitcase wrapped in plastic, even though she told him there was nothing valuable inside it, nor anything breakable. It was clearly an excuse to not have to wait with her, to get away from her, if only for ten minutes.

In the meantime, a girl had spat on her. A hyperactive little girl wearing thick makeup. The mother was reading a Greece holiday brochure and paying sparse attention to her child's acrobatics: the girl was leaping all over the seats like a chimpanzee. Then she sat down next to Ema, opened her mouth and fingered one of her wobbly teeth. 'Look! It moves!' Then she let a string of hot, thick drool fall from her mouth and land on Ema's arm.

Now, Ema picked up her suitcase and said thank you to Jerónimo, that he shouldn't have bothered. She expected him to say something else, but he just glanced at his watch and said, 'Right, it's about time.'

'Wait, please.'

Jerónimo looked at her with his mouth contorted, that expression that made his double chin lopsided, as if one side of his face weighed more than the other.

'What's wrong now?' he said impatiently.

He had also put on weight in the last few months. And he had no excuse.

'I don't know, I just don't like airports. I've never said goodbye to anyone, I don't know what it's like.' She felt like crying again.

'It's like this.' Jerónimo moved his hands around dementedly, like a mime waving. 'Bye.'

'I'd like to call you when I get there, would that be okay with you? So we can talk properly. I think we need to talk properly, and maybe doing it over the phone will help.'

Jerónimo now had his hands in his pockets and he raised his shoulders in that pose, the one that made his neck disappear. Jerónimo was full of tics, unnecessary movements, overdramatic gestures. Jerónimo was horrible. She was horrible too, and that shared characteristic should have been enough to make them revere one another.

'Ema,' he growled, 'I don't ever want to speak to you again, do you understand?' Ema shrugged, swallowed the lump in her throat. 'Go on, off you go.' He pointed towards the international departure gate.

The mother and the little girl were at the back of the queue. If she went now, she would bump into them again.

Jerónimo had bought her ticket the night before. It was the most expensive ticket in history: there were only business class seats left. He didn't care, he'd spent two months' salary and he couldn't care less.

'When you come back', said Jerónimo, 'I won't be in the apartment anymore.' He turned and hurried towards the exit before she could reply.

She went to join the queue. The little girl smiled at her, Ema blanked her and concentrated on the mother's magazine: *Discover Patmos*, said the front cover. In the background was a beach, and in the foreground, a couple in Greek dress. Jerónimo had once said that they would go to Greece. Not to Patmos; she couldn't remember where, but it would definitely have been somewhere more predictable, more picture-postcard. Ema told him that she didn't like places that were too beautiful.

He didn't understand. 'I hate beauty, that's why I love you,' she said to him, and reached out to stroke his face, but at that moment Jerónimo turned and she ended up poking him in the eye. 'Bitch!' he shouted. This made Ema so angry that, without thinking, she clenched her fist and punched him in the face.

★

She was woken by a noise on the roof. The sound of a heavy animal up there, a fox perhaps. It was given to scratching around on the flat roof and howling, as if begging for help. She sat up in bed. Her whole life she could remember this animal: when she was young she would cry with terror, but then she got used to it. Elsewhere, she heard somebody switch on a blender. Ema left her bedroom and made her way to the living room. There were four little water features, one in each corner of the room, which made the constant sound of a waterfall. Decorative metallic wind chimes tinkled in the windows. On the coffee table there was a fish bowl filled with coloured quartz pebbles instead of fish.

In the kitchen, her mother stood with her back to the door, blending something green. She had the cordless phone propped between her ear and her shoulder and was talking into it. Her voice hit Ema like the lash of whip, a sharp blow to the back of her neck.

'Emanuella always travels business class, and I think it's good that she does. She's been very stressed lately, with everything that's happened it's no wonder, the poor thing.'

'Mum?'

Her mother chucked the spinach leaves into the whirring blender and went on talking. She was wearing a dressing gown made out of Indian fabric. It showed her underwear; an enormous bra and a pair of tatty knickers. Ema sat down at the plastic dining table, leaned her elbows on the table top, her chin in her hands. The clock on the wall read nine o'clock. Years ago, her mother had sent her a wall clock similar to that one. It was made of transparent acrylic and filled with an iridescent liquid that changed colours as the hours went by. "Transform your fragility into something beautiful," said the card. Ema threw the clock in the bin without even taking it out of the box.

'...yes, she's better now, but she's still finding it hard to believe, we're all finding it hard. What a tragedy, my poor darling.' Her mother switched off the blender and turned around. When she saw Ema, her tone became serious, 'Let's talk later, my dear, bye.' She hung up.

She poured a glass of the green concoction and offered it to Ema, who shook her head.

'It's pure iron, try some, it'll do you good.' She guzzled down the liquid.

'Who were you talking to?' asked Ema.

Her mother washed up the glass. The water dribbled weakly out of the kitchen tap.

'What do you want for breakfast?'

Her mother was not really one for conversation. The things her mother said reflected her own train of thought, and nothing else.

'Coffee,' said Ema. 'Why did you say that I always travel business class? I've never travelled Business, it's like you're convinced that I'm Princess Caroline of Monaco or something.'

'I've got soya milk; do you want some?' Her mother took a carton out of the fridge. She opened it and was about to pour it into Ema's coffee.

'No, I don't want any of that.'

Her mother put the carton back in the fridge, brought her coffee over and sat down opposite her. 'Your aunt Ana has very strict visiting hours. I'm going to call the doctor now to see if we're allowed to go today, even if it's just for a short while. She'll be so happy to see you, she always asks after you, although she's a bit confused, poor thing.'

Ema blew on her coffee. Her mother had traces of green liquid at the corners of her mouth. She remembered the girl's dribble in the airport and felt repulsed. She pulled a napkin out of the napkin holder, which was shaped like a large plastic sunflower.

'Wipe your mouth,' she said, holding out the napkin, 'you've got green all over it.'

Her mother licked her lips. The green mark spread out but did not disappear.

'This juice is so good for your bowels, Emanuella, it helps you to digest undigestible things. It's a recipe I learned on that nutrition course. I told you about it, didn't I? The one from the magazine offer...'

'Yes, you told me.' Ema sipped her coffee.

Her mother was silent, as if she had forgotten the next line and was trying to remember it.

Ema hated it when she talked about bowels.

'Where's my dad?'

Her mother had picked up the remote control for the stereo system and was pointing it at it. Some kind of new age music started to play.

'I don't like it when you make up things about me,' Ema told her. 'I don't understand what you get out of lying to your friends about me.'

'I don't know what you're talking about, darling. Did you get out of bed the wrong side this morning?'

She stood up and went over to the kitchen counter, decanted the green liquid into a glass jar and put it in the fridge. Then she set about washing up the blender. Ema finished her coffee in three large swigs. The first burned her throat. The other two went down fine after that. In the cup, the dregs formed a messy shape. A nothing-y shape, a small brown heap without rhyme or reason. She got up from the table.

'I'm going for a shower.'

'Don't make any plans with anyone this afternoon, Emanuella.'

Who the hell was she going to make plans with? She didn't know anybody in that city. They had all left, like she had. Her mother had the phone in her hand again and was dialling a number.

'I'm not stressed, mum.'

Her mother was concentrating on the telephone keys. It seemed like she was dialling way more numbers than necessary, as if she was calling Tokyo. The blender was draining on the drying rack, creating a small green puddle underneath. Not as green as the juice; a diluted green. Her mother washed up badly. She had always washed up badly. There were always remains of things on the dishes: remnants of food, traces of soap, fingerprints in dried foam.

'Hello? Yes, I need to speak to Doctor Jaimes, please, I'm a relative of her patient, Ana Soto.' She picked up a dishcloth and wiped the counter top in circular movements. White rings still littered the surface: smears of old grease. 'Yes, of course, I'll hold.'

Ema remained standing in front of the plastic table. She touched her belly; it was a flabby, droopy mass of skin. In recent months, she had got used to the inflated feeling: it was like touching a water balloon, full to bursting. In recent months, Jerónimo would ask her things like, what does it feel like? And she'd reply, like I'm being squeezed. Or, what could it be doing? And she'd say, it's crushing my lungs, trying to suffocate me.

'I've never travelled business class. I hate it when you make up things about me. I hate it when you say anything about me.'

Her mother turned around; she was sweating heavily. She looked at Ema and raised her finger to her lips.

'Sshh.'

Ema went to have a shower.

★

She stepped out of the shower dripping wet. Her phone had been ringing for a while.

'Hello.'

It was Jerónimo. He did not know what to do with the baby clothes.

'Donate them to the Church,' she replied.

'You're the sickest person on earth.' He was crying.

Ema hung up. She imagined him drunk, foul-smelling.

The phone rang again. She wrapped her wet hair in a towel. Her head hurt.

'Hello,' she answered.

'I'm going to burn them.' He was raging.

She was naked and felt at a disadvantage. It seemed so unfair that he could just call her up whenever he wanted and assault her with everything that came into his head.

'Do whatever the fuck you want, I'm sick of hearing that victim voice of yours.'

'Am I not a victim?' Now he was laughing with that dry, cynical, fake laugh. 'What am I then?'

'…'

'You're happy.' He started crying again. 'You're relieved. It's so obvious that…'

'Drop dead.'

'You want me to die too? You need your head examined, you psycho.' He hung up.

Ema was shaking. She took the towel off her head and rubbed her hair. The mirror was where it had always been, hanging on the inside of the bedroom door. It still had some *Jem and the Holograms* stickers on it. She moved closer, stood up as straight as she could and looked at herself front on. Even in her most upright stance, she was hunched. And that belly, that damn flabby skin: the scar ran from one side to the other, reddish in colour. The stitches were badly done, it had ended up wonky, and this made the rest of her body look lopsided as well. Her boobs were swollen; she should have been breastfeeding right now. During the first days, when she expressed milk, she was worried that the stream would gush out so hard that her nipples would burst. She touched them, they were like rock: she pressed and expelled a trickle of whitish, watery liquid that ran down her belly and landed on the carpet.

'Emanuella?' Her mother opened the door.

Ema tried to shove her back, but she was already inside the room, looking at her with an expression that turned rapidly from pity to repulsion. Ema pushed her out of the room and pulled the door closed in her face.

'Sorry,' she managed to whisper from outside.

Ema heard her hurried footsteps down the corridor.

★

'Could you tell me where my dad is?'

Ema and her mother were in a taxi on the way to the psychiatric hospital. Her mother ignored her; she was busy giving directions to the driver. Absolutely unnecessary directions, seeing as it was the only psychiatric hospital in the city.

'Honestly, Emanuella, I don't want to get involved...'

'So don't then.'

'...but it's just that I find Jerónimo's attitude to be very inconsiderate.'

'Shut up.'

'Cruel, I'd say.'

'Sshh.' She covered her ears.

'...to leave now, when you need him most.'

Her mother rolled up the window, fanned herself with her hands.

'Can we have some air con please?' she asked the driver.

Ema also rolled her window up, but not all the way. She did not like feeling confined.

'I think that...'

'I don't care what you think.'

Her mother let out a deep sigh. After a short while she said, 'Anita's going to be so pleased to see you.'

She didn't even like her aunt Ana. She should have told her mother that, when she insisted on them going to visit her. 'She's your favourite aunt.' 'She's not my aunt, she's a dried-up old fossil.' But she was tired of arguing.

'I'm going to get an earlier flight back, mum,' said Ema.

Her mother, who had been silent, studying the taxi driver's information on the back of his seat, suddenly turned towards her. Her mouth was open and the look on her face was like a reaction to a different kind of sentence, such as 'I'm going to be sick on you, mum.' She was also sweating. For as long as Ema could remember, her mother had suffered from these sweats. She attributed it to 'a hormonal problem'. It was as if she'd been going through the menopause all her life: she was chronically menopausal.

'Do whatever you want, Emanuella.'

Her voice trembled, she looked out of the window, the glass reflecting her watery eyes.

Outside, a row of poplars lined the road. Poplars were not native to the area. A rather cultured mayor had introduced them from warmer climes and had them planted along the main avenues. The result was this tranquil, refined landscape, so at odds with the people who lived there.

The taxi pulled up outside the hospital. They got out, her mother rang the bell and a smiling nurse came out. They made their way down a dark corridor that stank of urine, until they reached the room where aunt Ana sat in her wheelchair. The walls were painted apple green, and there was an overpowering smell of medicine. Aunt Ana was made-up: a pair of red circles on her cheeks, and black pencil suggesting eyebrows she didn't have. She was balding. Her forehead was the worst; riddled with blue veins. Thin webs that looked like things underwater, drowned tentacles.

'She's still looking splendid, isn't she?' said her mother, nodding towards aunt Ana.

Ema nodded.

There was a single bed and a bedside table with a radio, and a picture of her, young and smiling, a large quiff adorning her face. She was neither ugly nor pretty. And, as far as Ema could recall, neither was she good at anything in particular. She was utterly unremarkable. Her mother, on the other hand, was very good at being mediocre at everything she did. She excelled at that: she put a lot of effort into being mediocre.

'Splendid,' her mother repeated. She hated lulls in conversation.

'It's because she never had children,' said the nurse.

Aunt Ana smiled as if they had paid her a compliment.

'Oh, but she did,' said Ema's mother, who was standing behind the wheelchair, raking through Ana's lank hair with her fingers, 'I mean, I was always like a daughter to her.'

Aunt Ana looked at her with expressionless eyes. Then she turned to Ema, who was standing in front of her. She clasped her wrist and pulled her in close, as if she wanted to tell her a secret:

'What did they do with the little body, Emanuella?'

Ema pulled away and looked at her mother, who cut in immediately. 'Look, Anita, what a beautiful day!' she exclaimed, pushing the wheelchair over to the window.

Ema sat down on the bed; the mattress was rock hard. Her heart was beating very fast and she felt a jabbing pain in her ribs. The nurse scrutinised her from the doorway. Ema held her gaze for a few seconds and then said, 'What are you looking at, you moron?'

★

That night she packed her bag and changed her return flight. In two hours the taxi would arrive to take her to the airport. She waited at the kitchen table, while her mother made fish stew, which smelled foul. She kept glancing at the acrylic clock. She still could not work out how she had ended up here. Jerónimo had come up with the idea one day, and she had not reacted fast enough. She'd said I don't know, maybe, and he'd dashed off to buy the ticket, to take her to the airport, to shoo her away like a mangy stray dog.

'It's a pity I didn't get to see my dad,' said Ema. 'Where have you got him hidden away?'

'Do you like mustard in it, Emanuella?'

Her mother held up the yellow jar, the spoon in her other hand, poised to dip.

Ema sighed and got up from the table. She crossed the living room, with its soundtrack of babbling water features, and went out the back of the house, to the garden: a dirt yard surrounded by a few bushes and dried leaves that nobody raked anymore. At the bottom was a shed of sorts, where they kept old junk. In the middle, there was a lantern and a stone bench that once served as the base for a little makeshift table using a piece of plywood. That is where she sat.

The little garden used to have a lovely, unobstructed view of the sky and poplars. Now a building had been erected behind it. The windows of the façade opposite were dotted with plastic flower pots and clothes hung to dry; the walls were grimy. The garden had been transformed into a cold, gloomy place. A place the sun no longer reached.

When she was little, Ema used to invite her school friends to have picnics in the little garden. Her mother would spread out a rug on the ground, and after they ate, they would lie there looking up at the clouds, singing songs, marrying boys from school. Once, at the beginning of everything, she had brought Jerónimo to her house. She showed him the little garden, which at that time still had an unobstructed view, and they lay on the ground to look at the clouds. He sung "Me and Bobby McGee" in a terrible accent. He said that the song was just like them. Ema thought that the song had nothing to do with them, but she nodded emphatically: 'It's true.'

The door of the shed opened. Her dad came out.

'Dad?'

Surprised, Ema stood up and moved towards him, but he instinctively took a step back, almost frightened.

'Emanuella,' he said.

He cleared his throat and smoothed down the thin fabric of his checked shirt. He looked unkempt; the right arm of his glasses was attached to the frames with sticky tape. He stuffed his hands in his trouser pockets and stared at the ground. Ema also looked at the ground. A line of ants was emerging from under a bush. It was marching its way across to the old dog kennel, which she had just noticed, stowed in a corner of the garden.

'Have you been here the whole time?' asked Ema.

Her father took a step forward, took off his glasses and wiped the lenses on his shirt. He put them away in his pocket.

'The thing is, I've made myself a little workshop.'

'What?'

'I don't know if your mum told you. I've taken up woodworking again, and well, I don't know.'

'What don't you know?'

He took a very deep breath.

'It's a very difficult situation for me, Em.'

'What situation?'

'I thought that your mum would do it better than me, and your aunt Ana, who you always loved so much. I wouldn't have known what to do, what to say to you.' He shook his head. 'Your attitude...' his voice faltered.

Ema felt a cold, metallic blow to the middle of her chest.

'You spoke to Jerónimo.'

Her father walked in the direction of the lantern.

'How did you get on today?'

As he walked past her, Ema smelled the familiar scent of cardamom cologne. She swallowed. 'It was fine,' she said.

Her father turned the bulb and the lantern lit up with a faint, yellowish glow. He took a cigarette out of his pocket and put it between his lips, unlit.

'I've booked a taxi to take me to the airport,' said Ema.

Her father nodded, sat down on the bench with his legs spread wide. It was a low bench; he looked like a frog. He slipped the cigarette into his shirt pocket and nodded in the direction of the building. 'Did you see that monstrosity that they've plonked there?'

'Yes.'

'It's an outrage, Em, don't you think? All those people looking into our back garden.' He shook his head, crestfallen. 'When they started building it, I tried to talk to the chief architect, he was a friend of one of Julio's cousins. Remember Julio?'

Ema nodded, her arms crossed tightly across her bust. It felt like her boobs were leaking again.

'That Julio was quite a character, but anyway, he got me an appointment with the architect and I went to see the guy, a real little toff, he was. He said yes, that I was right, blah blah blah… and when I asked him what he was going to do about it, he looked at me in surprise and said, "Oh, you want me to do something?"' He laughed.

Ema remembered him playing jokes on her, in the dining room: 'Look, Emanuella, a little purple bird!' and when she turned to look for the little purple bird, her father would quickly whisk a piece of meat or a chicken leg off her plate and onto his own.

'So, things have changed around here, Em,' he said,

looking straight at her, his eyes narrowed with age and short-sightedness, 'but not all that much.'

She went back to the bench and sat down next to him. She felt a burning sensation in her stomach and realised that, apart from the coffee that morning, she had not eaten anything all day.

'Why don't you tell me, Em?' he said, his voice a faint trickle. His hand tentatively brushed hers. 'Tell me what happened.'

Ema looked at the line of ants that ended inside the kennel. Or perhaps it started there and ended behind the bush. His question irritated her. It irritated her that he'd talked about her "attitude" before. It seemed intrusive to her. She felt his beady eyes boring into her cheek; that seemed intrusive as well. They were sitting so close together on that bench that if she decided to turn to face him, their noses would rub together.

'Emanuella!' He mother came out of the house.

They both turned to look at her. She was holding the cordless phone in one hand. Ema was sure she'd been spying on them and, when she saw that they had sat down to talk, she came hurtling out of the house. She stood in front of them, just far enough away so that she could stretch her arm out and not quite hit Ema in the face with the phone.

'It's Jerónimo.'

Ema took the phone, reluctantly, and held it to her ear. 'Hello.'

There was nobody there. Her parents had moved a few steps away with their backs to her, facing the building. In one of the windows there was a cat staring out into the void, a curtain fluttering behind it.

Her mother turned back to her and took the phone out of her hand.

'Everything alright, Emanuella?' she asked, already

walking back towards the house, without even waiting for an answer.

Before she went inside, she announced that the meal was ready, and to hurry up because it was going to get cold.

'Bloody ants.' Her dad was shaking the bottoms of his trousers.

Then he put his hand on her head and mussed up her hair, like a child. The light from the lantern illuminated him in detail. His face had the greyish hue of the elderly.

'Dad,' she said.

He turned to look at her, his eyes small and expectant once again. But she had nothing to say to him.

'Let's go.' He moved towards the house. 'Come on, Em, the food will be getting cold.'

PART III

SEXUAL EDUCATION

1

Moisture

'In girls, just like in other fauna, moisture attracts all sorts of nasties.' Olga Luz was pacing from one end of the classroom to the other, her gaze fixed on an invisible point somewhere above our heads. She walked in a straight line, always the same path. As if she was afraid of getting lost, or was already lost.

'Are we talking about any kind of moisture?' She had an odd habit of answering her own questions. 'Yes. And sweat too?' She shook her head. Her hands were folded over her stomach. 'Sweat too, but the other kind of moisture in particular.'

Dalia and I were writing notes to each other in our exercise books, but Olga Luz hadn't noticed. We weren't talking, because Olga Luz was very sensitive to whispering. She had a trained ear: she must have spent hours listening at closed doors.

'Friction doesn't help, quite the opposite in fact. For example, if you're dancing with a boy and you get moist down there, and the boy also gets moist down there, it's very likely that some creepy-crawly will sneak out of his moisture and cling to your skirt. From there it'll get into to your moist underwear and then inside you, like a fish that, after suffering in an inhospitable environment, returns to the sea. To its habitat. And although put like that it might seem like a fish in the sea is the most natural and inoffensive thing in the world, sometimes it isn't. There are some fish that make the sea rotten.'

I had a fish once. It was called Julia. Or Julio.

It is hard to tell the sex of a fish before they are a year old. Mine didn't make it to three months. Cleaning out a fish tank is a laborious job.

I drew Julia in Dalia's exercise book.

Dalia drew a circle around it. She added stick arms and legs to the circle, and a microcephalic head.

Olga Luz's skirt came to halfway down her calves. Her ankles looked too puny to support the weight of her body. She wasn't fat, but she was big-boned, with sturdy, cylindrical hips. When she stood there in front of us, she reminded me of an old cabinet with warped legs that my grandma used to have in her living room.

'Ancient Egyptian sages discovered a method for preventing moisture in the areas we were talking about.'

And you will make of your vulva a desert, I wrote to Dalia in the exercise book, and Dalia covered her mouth to stifle a laugh, but it was too late.

'What's so funny, Dalia?' Olga Luz glared at her with her tormented look. The whites of her eyes were little more than thin rings around the dark, over-dilated irises.

Dalia cleared her throat and said that she thought the fish metaphor was very distasteful, because it was like accepting the sexist myth about women smelling bad.

Nobody laughed.

Or worse, Dalia continued, it was like propagating the myth, like saying that we smelled that way because inside us we had an army of prodigal fish returning to the sea to their – she made inverted commas in the air with her fingers – "habitat". And that was the same as saying we smelled like that because we were sluts.

It was the first Tuesday in March.

This incident got Dalia placed on disciplinary probation, and the rest of us got a warning.

Luckily it was also the last year of school, in other words the only possible punishment was for them to withhold the diploma for a while: without a diploma, we could not go to university. But Dalia didn't want to go to university. Dalia wanted to hit the road with nothing but a rucksack and travel all the way down to Patagonia and then come back up and go all the way to Mexicali, Baja California. How many times? Until she carved a furrow in the ground. She'd been going on about this idea for about a year. During the last holidays she had grown dreads and her hair smelled of rotten egg. She'd also given up shaving her legs, and went around in short skirts, showing her pale calves bristling with curly black hairs. One night, her dad chopped off her dreadlocks with scissors while she was sleeping, and the next morning she had to dash to a hairdresser, where they gave her a bowl-cut. Following that, she bought some fake thick-framed glasses. That year she would end up going for the John Lennon look. From behind those glasses she was now staring defiantly at Olga Luz, who simply jotted something down in her notebook for later, then turned on her heel and left the room.

In the next class, the rules were intensified. Olga Luz prohibited any form of intervention apart from nodding in silence; we were not even allowed to get out our notebooks and/or pencils. Why did we need them? Important lessons were retained in the mind, and the *most* important were retained in the flesh. Punishable acts included whispering, sneezing or yawning. If any of those occurred, Olga Luz would put a mark by your name on a list. Three marks equalled disciplinary probation. Others – me included – did care about the diploma. Others – me included – thought that backpacks and dreads and Latin American travels were an invention of poor people who liked to think they were bohemians. Dalia was not poor, but she smoked weed and that was enough to make her feel bohemian. Of course, she also loved her automatic pickup truck, with its booming sound system. We would drive around the city in the pickup, burning rubber, and caterwauling: *And the sky was all violet!*

My mum hated Dalia, among other reasons because every time I went out with her, somebody would call her to say that they'd seen me in an outlandish pickup truck, with my hair all wild, clutching a bottle and singing ungodly things.

The teachers weren't that fond of her either; the thing about the disciplinary probation was no surprise to anyone. Olga Luz had already described Dalia once as the epitome of the "bad apple". She was right: Dalia's powers of persuasion could only have been bestowed on her by the devil himself. And it's not like she even had to make much effort; it came naturally to her. Like when we met up in the kitchen courtyard after lunch – a secluded spot where the teachers rarely went, making it the ideal smoking hideaway – and she would start regaling us with her dreams. Because dreaming was a sin, but a minor one. It was not the same as having bad thoughts when you were awake. That's why our dreams were the ideal location for sucking out the venom implanted in our heads by our school teachers. I dreamed too, but I could rarely remember what about. I only remembered the sensation that lingered in my body: a mixture of happiness and repulsion that was a real pain in the ass to deal with. Dalia said that she could remember all her dreams perfectly and could reproduce them in detail. So, we would all lie back on the rough concrete, with the kitchen extractor fan whirring away noisily in the background.

Once she dreamed that Mr Tomasito – the guy who cleaned the school's roof and the gutters where the leaves and lizards gathered – raped Lucía, a classmate who had joined in ninth grade and had never really managed to fit in. In the dream, Mr Tomasito was standing on the roof in nothing but a pair of Speedos, wearing a gold cape that fluttered behind him. All of us – students and teachers – were looking at him from below as he stood stock still, hands on his hips, staring down at his boner, which grew and grew until it burst out of his swimming trunks. But it did not stop there: Mr Tomasito's dick slithered down like a snake and chased after us. Terrified, we hurtled through the gardens and climbed the trees, shrieking. At some point Lucía tumbled face first out of one of the trees, but she didn't hurt herself because, thanks to her massive tits, she bounced back up. In that moment, Mr Tomasito's dick pounced on her, coiled itself around her waist, darted in between her legs and wham! It skewered her. That seemed to be the end of it, but it wasn't. Mr Tomasito's giant dick snake then forced its way up through Lucía's innards – her belly, guts, stomach, gullet, throat – and burst out of her mouth, wrapped itself around her tits (to do so, it had to make an extremely pronounced curve) and bam! It shot its load. Its semen was not milky white, but dark, black and oily, like he was.

Total silence.

I think even the noise of the extractor fan stopped at that moment. But as always, someone shattered the peace by stating the obvious.

'Bullshit. You didn't dream that.'

And Dalia laughed, proud of her invention which was totally crazy and filthy, although much more feasible than anything dreamt up by Olga Luz.

So that was Dalia: a bad apple.

She was also my best friend, and the only reason she

hadn't been kicked out was because she did well at school; and because her mother was dead, and because her dad was a big deal in the city, a member of the Conservative party. This man always wore a long-sleeved shirt buttoned right up the neck. Dalia told me it was because he had a burn scar. 'Doesn't he get really hot?' I asked her. She said he didn't, because before he got dressed he would cover himself in Mexsana medicated talc. I would think of the sticky clumps of it all over the guy's chest, and even saying hi to him from a distance made me feel sick.

Anyway, the point is that because of Dalia we spent a good part of our final year listening to Olga Luz prattling on about the virtues of the hymen and the unspeakable dangers of semen. Olga Luz hated semen so much that she would never call it semen. The few times she had to refer, for example, to an ejaculation, she would call it 'the substance that spills out of men's members.' And she wrinkled up her nose, as if she could smell her own bad breath.

Her class was part of an experimental project that was being piloted with my school year: instead of the sex education classes that had been mandatory in schools since 1993, they made us take an abstinence course, imported from Medellín and before that, Washington. The course was called *Teen Aid*. On the first day of *Teen Aid*, three years ago now, some provincial Barbie pumped full of silicone and dressed in pink came to tell us how healthy and *cool* abstinence was. She said it in a tone of voice bordering on soft porn. Then we watched some videos of the parents who founded *Teen Aid* – a red-haired, plump, freckly couple – booming an enthusiastic slogan on-screen: *Abstinence is saying yes to the rest of your life!* All the teaching material for the course – reams of glossy, coloured paper – was in English, because at my school even the signs in the chapel were in English: *Sshh, God is watching.*

The exercises we did as part of *Teen Aid* were like those quizzes you get in Cosmopolitan magazine, simulating very specific dangerous situations, in great detail. Some had illustrations representing the sexual act – a dotted line leading to the edge of a volcano, emanating noxious gases – a circumstance preceded by moments of increasingly intense wetness. Like the dew creeping over a window on a winter's morning, moisture spread throughout girls' bodies until they were just a pair of trembling legs bogged down in a swamp, which before that was a pool, and before that a waterfall, and before that a small stream, and before that barely a slow drip that was born and died between their legs.

Gross.

This allusion to teenage horniness, besides being twisted, was just gross.

The answers to the tests were multiple choice style, and your choices would place you somewhere in the psyche-delic maze that accompanied the exercise: a whirlpool of colour that would lead you to happiness or unhappiness, depending on what path you chose. You could end up at unhappiness through sheer carelessness. Any silly little decision could end up being catastrophic: like accepting a beer from a sweet, smiling guy – a blond, blue-eyed Jason Priestley type – who, it turned out, was actually a pervert, who pulled you into a dark corner and whispered in your ear and made your knickers moist. And from moist knickers, we all knew, only bastard babies came. Like moss spores. Happiness, on the other hand, was reached by a one-way path: straight, luminous, and as dry as an old bread roll. Being happy was easy.

2

Catechism

Next to the school was the Botanical Garden. Sometimes, with Dalia and other girls from our year, we would break into it by climbing over a barbed wire fence. To do what? To smoke, drink, take off our school pinafore dresses, tan our legs. There wasn't much sun there, however, because right in the part that adjoined the school the sky was blocked out by tree branches. Millions of tiny green leaves that quivered like insects, but every so often a wind would blow, opening a gap in them and we would be bathed in an intense light, as if God himself had opened the universal photon tap to baptise us again.

We would make our escape during second break, when the teachers shut themselves away in their offices. They claimed they were marking exam papers, but really, they went for a nap. It was obvious, because afterwards they would come out looking bleary-eyed and with their hair – usually so shiny and pulled tight to their head – all dishevelled.

One afternoon in early April, I climbed over into the Botanical Garden with Dalia, Marcela and Karina. Before Dalia, Marcela had been my best friend, but when the four of us started going around together, it became clear that Dalia and I shared something special, which neither she nor Karina would ever understand. Marcela started spending more time with the girls from the Olympic gymnastics group she trained with, and only really hung out with us when we went to the Botanical Garden. Karina was a necessary accessory to the group: we liked her, but above all we needed her. Karina had the unanimous and undisputed approval of all the teachers. Being with her was a guarantee that, however badly we behaved, the punishment would never be taken to its extreme.

That day we entered by our usual route and reached a clearing in the wood, with a natural pool in the middle of it. In one corner was a little grotto, and in the grotto was a Virgin adorned with rotting flowers and a mass of worms. May was over a month away; nobody had bothered to replace the flowers yet. Karina scurried over to clean her up. Karina was a real devotee of Mary: she had convinced everyone that the Virgin talked to her in her sleep and gave her instructions about how to behave at moments of moral conflict. We'd already heard about her dilemmas a thousand times. Sometimes they were things as silly as whether she should pinch her little brothers on the napes of their necks, like feral dogs, or if she should praise them, like healthy growing human beings. Karina could be exhausting, and the Virgin was her crutch, her last resort, her rhetorical amulet, her dildo.

Marcela, Dalia and I lay down in the grass and lit a Belmont menthol, which didn't smell as strong as Marlboros.

I never smoked again after I left school, but back then, lighting up a cig was like a rebellion hidden in my body, without running too much of a risk of being expelled. It was like saying: I swallow this poison and I exhale it back out into the world. Because the world deserves it.

Marcela had spent ages trying to prove to us that the song 'Angel' by Aerosmith was riddled with subliminal messages, but she was having trouble flipping the phrase from the chorus around and saying it backwards:

Thginot em evas dna emoc, legna ym er'uoy!

When Karina came back from sprucing up the Virgin, she sat down cross-legged, her back straight, with that "it-wasn't-me" look on her face. She smoothed down the folds of her skirt with her hands and said:

'The Virgin spoke to me again yesterday.'

I found it funny that she said it like it was something extraordinary. It wasn't. According to Karina, the Virgin communicated with her practically every day.

'I bet she was bad-mouthing Steve Tyler,' Dalia said. Marcela and I laughed. Karina ignored her and continued:

'So, I had asked her what I should do with Chubby Arias.' As she talked, she scraped the pink varnish off her nails, creating a little heap of it on the grass. 'He keeps on about us going to his island, just the two of us, but I think that if I say yes, I'm going to regret what happens there…'

'His island is *actual* paradise,' sighed Marcela.

It was true, I'd been there once: a plot of land with the house in the middle of it, and huge picture windows overlooking the sea on one side and a forest of bamboo on the other. Half the girls in our year had gone out with Chubby Arias just because he had an island. And a yacht called Elvira. Elvira was his mother, a Chilean divorcee who all the other mothers said was too liberal. My mum attributed this to where she came from: she said that the further down the continent you went, the more shameless the women. Modesty was a virtue that existed on a sliding scale, starting out in Mexico and going to absolute pieces in Argentina. Colombia was located, conveniently, slap bang in the middle.

A year ago, Chubby Arias had celebrated his eighteenth birthday on the island with a massive party. It kicked off early, in the morning, and went on all day. Dalia and I came back at midnight on a boat specially hired for the occasion. We had gone with Karina, but at the last minute we lost her in the forest. At that time, Chubby Arias was dating a girl in one of the years below; her name was Inés and she acted like she was royalty. But at the party, she must have been humiliated to see her boyfriend touching up every female who came over to him: 'Hey Chubby!' 'Happy Birthday, Chubster!' 'You handsome devil, Chubby, get over here!' Chubby Arias groped people here, kissed people there, swigging from a bottle of Old Parr the whole time. At one point, Inés went over to retrieve him, and Chubby showed her who was boss by giving her a couple of slaps on the cheek. Not hard, but forceful. The girl retreated into a corner clutching a tall, brightly coloured drink and that was the last we saw of her. Next thing we knew, Karina, as if she had been poised, waiting for that moment, suddenly took centre stage. We saw her absolutely going for it on the dance floor, bowing and scraping at Chubby Arias' feet like he was the Holy Spirit incarnate.

There was a DJ, and Elvira kept on going up to request songs he'd never heard of. The most disturbing thing about the party must've been the point when Elvira danced with her son, a kind of electronic courtship dance that required them to grind up and down, back to back, with their hips swirling like tornadoes. Although Dalia and I found it highly inappropriate, the rest of the guests, Karina included, seemed to find it funny. They clapped. They laughed so hard they choked. They flirted with Chubby, who was an absolute babe magnet on the dance floor. And off the dance floor. What was so charming about him? Honestly, I'll never work it out. He had never been my boyfriend; I was not deemed worthy of being in his social circle. Also, the one and only time he tried to say hi to me, which was on the night of the party, I swerved out of his way and turned my back on him.

'What's the matter?!' he shouted, 'Do I smell, or what?'

He grabbed my arm and swung me round to face him, blocking my way. In fact, he did smell terrible, but that was the least of his flaws.

'Can't we talk?' he insisted. His speech was slurred, his breath toxic, his face sweaty like a greased pig.

I said no. He asked why not.

I thought about my reply. I tried to summon up some shred of tactfulness, weighing up the possibilities of that mansion in the middle of the Caribbean Sea, and the yacht Elvira, with its wooden deck and soft, velvet-cushioned seats; weighing up the advantages of having a friend who was repulsive but rich. Whether the lovely sailing trips for me and my friends would somehow make up for his absolute lack of manners.

'Because talking to you is like dunking my head in a bucket of vomit.'

So long, sucker!

'…We've already done some stuff, but not all of it,' Karina continued with her story, although nobody was paying much attention to her, 'he knows that I believe in virginity and he respects that, but I like him so much that it's become a really hard penance.'

'What did the Virgin say to you?' I asked her.

Karina mumbled something that I couldn't hear. Then she cleared her throat, as if she was about to say something, but didn't.

'What did she say?' I repeated.

I hate people who play at being mysterious, it was

obvious that she was going to tell us, it was obvious that she was dying to tell us, but she wanted us to beg.

'Well,' she took a deep breath: 'She told me that my virginity was very important, but that didn't mean we couldn't do other things…'

'Blah blah,' said Dalia, 'tell me something I don't know.'

'Yeah,' said Marcela, 'even my mum told me that, and she can't even remember being a virgin.'

'Your mum told you that?' asked Dalia.

Marcela took a drag of the Belmont and replied in a cloud of smoke:

'It's a figure of speech.'

'…and she also told me,' Karina continued, 'that we must safeguard the hymen, but that there are other parts of the body we can make love with.'

This left us speechless. I wasn't sure if I had understood. I'm not sure if Dalia and Marcela had either.

'She said "safeguard"?' I asked her, just to break the silence. But also because I felt that the Virgin, even though Karina had made her up, wouldn't talk like that.

Karina shrugged. It was her turn to smoke: she inhaled deeply and blew it out. Her face was hidden behind a veil of smoke.

'Yeah, I don't know. I can't remember.'

The Virgin had told Karina that Chubby Arias could do her up the ass. Dalia confirmed this later, over the phone. I told her she was crazy. And she told me that it wasn't the first time that Chubby had suggested doing that with girls. Some of them had told her: the ones who said no, the ones who thought that it was not only a sin, but that it was also disgusting. Chubby Arias insisted that it wasn't a sin and even brought along a book of catechism to back up his argument. He had highlighted a quotation from Saint Ambrose about the virtues of chastity: "There are three forms of the virtue of chastity: the first is that of spouses, the second that of widows, and the third that of virgins." From there, he drew an arrow to the margin, with a definition of virginity as: "the quality of possessing an intact hymen and not a perforated hymen." A definition which he then interpreted: the only thing that must remain intact is the hymen, everywhere else has free reign, a blessed gift from our Lord God. Who are we to spurn God's gifts? The body should be used to please Him, to say: Thank you, take this broken ass as a sign of my blessed devotion to you, Jesus Christ.

Chubby Arias was like one of those psychos who came round knocking door-to-door spouting catechism, with their little annotated books, and their fake morals. He must have convinced Karina, or perhaps they'd already done it, and that's why she was going around telling that story about the Virgin. The image of Karina in a submissive posture, with that greaseball delving into her from behind like a nosebag, was too much for me.

'Ugh,' I said to Dalia. 'He's such a perv.'

'But his theory has merit.'

'Maybe,' I said. But I thought that if you pulled out any loose phrases from the catechism and stitched them together, any theory would have merit. I realised that this was the purpose of catechism. The darkest mysteries – the Holy Trinity, the Immaculate Conception, the Holy Grail – all became much clearer after being doctored by some con man who wanted something in return: a bag of coins, divine grace, Karina's ass. It was all the same.

3

Broken Girls

Dalia was becoming obsessed with her Latin America trip and it was pissing me off. She was constantly producing a fold-out map, which took up too much space on the desk in the library where I was studying. I asked her not to disturb me; I needed to concentrate. She used the fold-out map to tell me things, although a minute earlier I had expressly asked her to kindly shut up. She lifted it up by the top corners, over her head: behind it I could see the silhouette of her head as a backdrop to the Pacific Coast. She talked and talked, and when I complained, she said:

'Just imagine that my voice is a buzzing insect.'

'A cicada... no, a hornet. A horny hornet.'

That wound her up after the weekend she'd had: she had been hanging around in Bocachica and met some guys who had travelled through Peru, Bolivia and Chile, playing in an Andean fusion band, and who now ran a tattoo shop. The singer was called Blas; I saw him for the first time at a gig that Dalia took me to. 'Hey, babe,' he said right into my ear, his hot breath reeking of weed. I didn't like him. But Dalia insisted, and I went with her a couple more times to meet up with those guys.

The second time we saw them was at the tattoo shop, which was where they rehearsed. She'd hooked up with a guy called J, who was the drummer and the guy in charge of everything: the band, the shop and the wasters that used to hang out there, smoking weed and generally kissing his ass. That time, J and Dalia flopped onto a grubby sofa and started kissing and fondling each other, and everyone seemed to think that it was totally normal. I went to sit on a bench outside on the pavement, because I was embarrassed at the display they were putting on. Blas followed me out.

'What do you want?' I said to him.

The guy sat down next to me and started whistling a song by *Los Enanitos Verdes*. After a little while, I heard Dalia shouting, crying for help and hurling insults at J. When I went inside, she was standing in the middle of the shop, with her shirt ripped, one tit hanging out:

'You son of a bitch, I told you to stop!'

Dalia had hickeys all over her neck, chest and belly. She looked like she had been attacked by leeches. J had a scratch on his face and a bitemark with broken blood vessels on his arm.

'Prick tease!' he yelled at her.

And the others? It was as if they were listening to rain falling. The guy on the maracas hadn't missed a beat.

I told Dalia we should go.

'I'm not going anywhere until this fucker pays for my shirt.' She stood there with her arms crossed, hips tilted. Her tit was like an accessory she was wearing; nobody seemed bothered by it. J looked at her furiously, but suddenly he smiled like a psycho and said that if he got her on her own one day, he would rape her.

'Go to hell, the lot of you,' I muttered, and I left.

I thought that Dalia would follow me, but when I reached the corner I looked back, and she was nowhere to be seen. But who was there? That guy Blas. He gestured for me to wait, and he jogged up to me at a cool pace, one which seemed to say, 'I could easily follow you for half a block without breaking a sweat, babe.'

'Where's Dalia?' I said.

Blas took a joint out of his pocket and tucked it behind his ear. Then he suggested we go to the kiosk to get something to drink.

'Like what?'

'Whatever, it's hot.'

Every time the guy opened his mouth, a waft of marijuana hit me. I didn't like weed. I didn't like any drugs, but above all, I'd rather dive head-first into a pool filled with anthrax than take a drag on some crusty hippy's joint.

The kiosk was on the other side of the street. I was thirsty, so I crossed over with Blas. I ordered a Sprite and he ordered a Coke. We said nothing for a while, watching the buses and the street hawkers going up and down San Martín Avenue. Nobody was in a hurry in that city, rather the opposite: everyone walked around as if their own shadows were weighing them down.

'Where do you live?' he asked me.

I shrugged. 'Somewhere over there.'

In those days I was living with my grandma because my mum and my sister Juana were in Medellín. Juana had paid for the trip. Juana had money because she'd spent the last few months working as a secretary for an oil company; she had already given up on three different degrees and a language course and wasn't going to study anymore. What was the point, she said, if she was already earning a salary? I, on the other hand, spent all day long with a book in my hands, though I wasn't really studying that hard. I skim read, and that was enough to make my mum happy. She was always nagging me about my grades.

The thing is, my family weren't that well-off during those years, and although the most logical solution would have been for me to switch to a cheaper school – like the one Juana had gone to – my mum was set on me getting a scholarship. And they gave me one, the sole condition being that I had to maintain an average grade of 9 or above. That was no big deal, it was an easy school: the teachers were more concerned with what they called "spiritual education" than in any of us learning the periodic table. But all the same, I didn't want to give my mum any reason to say it was my fault that we were poor, so I laid it on thick with the sacrifice I was making; constantly clutching my books and shutting myself away to study, to achieve the bare minimum to keep my average at 9.1: no more, no less.

Our final year was a bit harder because I was going to enrol in a public university and I had to get good marks in the national exams. I had to study properly for that. Other classmates of mine were going off to study in the United States and were more concerned with their TOEFL scores. And others were going to Bogotá, to private universities where all you needed to get in was money. All those girls cared about was being skinny: they dedicated entire breaks to studying the calorific value of a Snickers bar. And they were skinny, and they were tanned. At the weekends they went to the islands to eat and to throw up. They got blind drunk, dabbled in drugs, boyfriend-swapped and safeguarded their hymens.

I couldn't stand them.

But back then, I couldn't really stand anyone.

Not my friends, not my mum, not my sister Juana.

My father got off lightly in that respect, because he had left a long time ago and you can't pick fights with people who aren't there. The thing with my sister was more complicated. In a nutshell: word was going around that my sister was a bit of a slut. Well, that's what I heard people were saying at school. Actually, that's what Dalia told me people were saying at school. Because nobody would dare say it to my face. Not because they were embarrassed or felt sorry for me, but because they were afraid of how I would react. If anybody came up to me and said, 'I heard your sister's a slut,' I'd tell them, 'Well, I heard that every morning your mum pops three unripe bananas up her pussy and when she takes them out they're cooked, that's how much of a horny bitch she is. And do you know what she does with them after? I heard she mashes them up and serves them to you for breakfast.' If they tried to dob me in to any of the teachers, simple: I denied everything.

'Can you explain it to me?'

He was a real broken record, that guy. And so basic. He'd been banging on at me about the same thing for ages: about why the girls from my school were such a bunch of prick-teasing princesses, so handsy but never putting out, such frigid clams. I'd decided to ignore him, so I didn't end up swearing at him. I didn't know him well enough to risk it; he could easily punch me in the face and break my nose, and I wasn't about to make my grandma come rushing out to the hospital.

'Well?' said Blas.

I downed my Sprite.

The afternoon was like all afternoons: hot, humid, and it dragged.

I looked over at the door of the shop. A Jamaican mobile hung in the doorframe: little black wooden figurines that knocked against one another, making a rattling noise. Dalia still hadn't come out.

Teen Aid was actually a measure that the school had been forced to take out of desperation, to stem the tide of pregnant pupils in recent years. The women who held our religious classes and retreats, who were from Opus Dei – the order that ran the school – were far too modest to dare talk about the things that *Teen Aid* could deal with so naturally, and in English, which made it all the more palatable. Everyone at our school had witnessed at some point or other some girl in tenth grade, ninth even, coming in to school after a few days of absence, dressed in home clothes, accompanied by her parents and with terrifying bags under her eyes like a concentration camp victim. We had all seen her going into the headmistress's office, and her parents traipsing after her, tragic and resigned, as if she were about to be burned alive in there and there was nothing they could do about it. The headmistress, however, showed leniency: she demanded a swift, no-frills wedding and offered for the school to take care of the baby, at no cost. The future mother came out of there at peace with the world, ready to deliver the child into the care of Opus Dei. *The End.*

But as the same story kept on repeating, rumours started spreading about a nursery that they were going to have annexed to the school, exclusively for the children of ex-pupils. One resentful newspaper columnist – according to the headmistress – wrote an article blaming the school for the girls' pregnant bellies, for putting it into their heads that taking contraceptives was the same as abortion, and it was clear that for a Catholic girl to have an abortion was equivalent to mutilating the baby Jesus with a pair of pliers. Then along came *Teen Aid*, spreading its militant message of abstinence. Honestly, I thought that it was better than the crazy teenage baby boom which left you no way out other than permanently giving up, firstly, your free will and choice (they wouldn't let you even choose your own underwear after that), and secondly, your untimely offspring.

Just as I was about to explain this to Blas, I heard the

wooden mobile rattling and I glanced over: Dalia and J were coming out of the shop. Lucky, I thought, because I was only going to waste my breath. Guys like Blas would never understand something like that. Guys like Blas had brains that were fried by smoking weed and all they knew about women was that they had a hole between their legs: if that hole was closed, all that was left was a useless piece of flesh surrounding it. When it came down to it, Blas was only wasting his precious weed breath on me because he hoped to split me in half like a ripe papaya. His persuasive strategy was as dumb as the women from *Teen Aid*.

Once, on Juana's birthday, a similar discussion arose. When she told her friends which school I went to, there were sounds of general disapproval. And a long-haired guy with a face like a Border Collie piped up, saying that at my school they thought women were like buckets: if they were broken, they were useless. Juana and her friends – who had surely all been broken since the day they were conceived – applauded the comment and made faces like they felt redeemed. I felt embarrassed for them. I thought that if these girls needed some shaggy-looking halfwit to leap to their defence with an analogy like that, it was because deep down they felt flawed, incomplete, battered, crippled.

Broken.

Buckets.

On the pavement outside, Dalia put her hands on J's chest and laughed. She looked satisfied, smitten. She was hot to trot. She had changed out of her shirt and into a black T-shirt that was far too small for her: Tweety Pie's face was stretched over her bust. I wondered if perhaps J had a daughter. They said goodbye with an over-the-top kiss. I imagined J's tongue darting down her throat like a severed tentacle and I shuddered. Then Dalia beckoned me over to get in the truck.

4

Lucía (and Mauricio)

I woke with a start, from a dream that I immediately forgot. It took me a while to remember why I was sleeping there in that hammock strung up between two posts. Above me was a canopy of dry palm trees that let very little light through. Barely a few thin rays, like knitting needles. A buzzing insect was hovering very close to my face. Where was I? At Lucía's place in the country. Why was I there? Because in the last few weeks Dalia and I had fallen out and Lucía had become my most loyal friend.

Lucía and her boyfriend, Mauricio.

I got up and went to the toilet. As I was about to leave the bathroom, I heard a noise from outside; it sounded like the rustle of clothing against clothing. I wiped the edge of the bidet with toilet paper, climbed up and grabbed the window frame. I peered out of the small high window with a screen over it, which looked out onto the verandah where Lucía and Mauricio were finishing off the game of Monopoly I had abandoned.

Lucía's shirt was pulled up, showing her incredibly white tits, bigger than I'd imagined, with tiny, pinkish nipples. Mauricio was sucking on one of her nipples with his eyes closed, using one hand to knead her tits and the other to touch her under her skirt. Lucía had her gaze fixed on the door through which her mother might appear if she woke up from her nap. She had her legs spread, hanging off the arm of the lounger. Her hands were clenched into fists, but then she pushed Mauricio's head down and he went under her skirt and held her thighs open with his hands. I could hear what sounded like a dog licking something. Lucía was making short, sharp movements with her hips; she jerked up and down as if she was gnawing away down there with tiny chipmunk teeth, as if she was trying to swallow Mauricio's entire head in little nibbling motions. I tried to stand on tiptoe to get a better look, but I almost lost my balance and was afraid I was going to fall. I carefully climbed down off the bidet and sat on the toilet.

Two weeks earlier, the scene was radically different:

My grandma was snoring in front of the TV. Armando Manzanero was playing piano on the theme tune to an afternoon TV soap that they repeated at midnight. When I turned the TV off, my grandma opened her eyes and raised her hand to her chest.

'I dreamed about your mother,' she got out of the rocking chair and headed for the phone. 'I'm going to call her.'

'My mum's not there, grandma.'

She turned to look at me.

'Oh no?

But she picked up the phone anyway, sat down on the sofa and dialled a number. Just one. Then she fell asleep again, with the phone to her ear.

I had just got home from a night out with Dalia and other girls from my year. Dalia had talked us into going to one of J's gigs at a bar in town called Zarathustra. It was one of those dingy dive bars that reek of piss. The crowd were, basically, skanks. I told Dalia that I thought J and his band were gross and she got annoyed.

'You think everyone's gross,' and she turned away from me.

I left. The other girls had gone to play on the slot machines at the end of the bar.

On the way back to my grandma's house I went over two bridges: the one that divided the centre from Manga, and Manga from La Popa; that part of the city was a succession of bridges that linked the neighbourhoods separated by inlets of the bay. I liked walking around there because it was like looking inside the city, with the lights on both sides of the water. But people said that at night, rapists hid in the mangroves and would pounce on you like jaguars at the slightest provocation. So, I ran as fast as I could over the bridges and kept on running until I reached the door of the house. I was panting, in a cold sweat.

My room was the ironing room.

I went into my room and stuck my head out of the window. There was nobody on the neighbouring balcony, which had bars around it. My window had a screen, but it was always open because otherwise the hot air got trapped inside and created a microclimate where the flies frazzled to death. A couple of years ago, the neighbouring balcony didn't have any bars on it, and some retarded kid who lived there threw himself off. He hit his head so hard that he ended up more deranged than he was to begin with. Now he could no longer hurl himself off it, but he would come out onto the balcony, grip the bars and howl with laughter. Sometimes he spent hours sadly staring out at La Popa hill. Sometimes he shouted swear words and his mother would whack him over the head with a shoe. But today he wasn't there. Where might he be? Sleeping, surely. Dreaming about dying and leaving that pathetic life he'd been dealt, to go straight to heaven. My grandma had told me that the boy's mother consoled herself with the myth that her son was an angel on earth. This annoyed my grandma: 'If heaven is full of retards, I'd rather go to hell.'

The phone rang. My grandma didn't hear it, although she was sitting right next to it, fossilised. I came out of my room to answer it:

'Hello.'

'Bitch.' It was Dalia.

According to her, I'd left her in a dangerous situation, which meant I was despicable and selfish. Apparently, the gig had got out of control. Someone had thrown a chair at J's back and they had ended up in Accident and Emergency. She had left him there, hugging an old woman in animal print leggings who, it turned out, was his mother.

'What about the other girls?' I yawned. I had sat down on the floor and was studying my grandma's feet, which were covered in swollen veins and brown moles.

'They cleared off as soon as it started getting rowdy in there.'

'So go and give them a hard time; at least I told you I was leaving.'

I took off my sandals and looked at my own feet, criss-crossed with veins that were still flat. My nails were long, they needed cutting. The skin on my feet was darker than on my calves, because I went round in flip-flops and jeans, so they caught the sun. Whenever I put shorts on, it looked like I had khaki-coloured ankle socks on.

'...you're my best friend, you should have stayed with me until the end.' It sounded like Dalia was about to cry. In those days, nothing annoyed me more than people crying. I told her to think of it as a practice run.

'A practice run for what?'

'For your trip to Patagonia.'

'How do you mean?'

'Or were you thinking of taking me as a chaperone for

when you're hooking up with your crusty boyfriends?'

'Bitch.'

'You're going to be alone on that trip, dealing with the scum.'

'You've got such a fucking chip on your shoulder.'

'And you're a skank.'

I hung up.

The situation got worse over the next few days. Dalia wasn't talking to me and started hanging around with girls who spent all day slurping on a Snoopy thermos filled with rum and Coke. Then they went out to the playground and did burping competitions until they fell asleep. They slipped Mr Tomasito some money on the sly, to make sure that the teachers didn't come and interrupt their nap.

I threw myself into my studies, I was dreaming bigger than public university: I wanted a scholarship to join NASA and slide off the edge of the map forever. Ugh. I spent all my time alone, finding shady spots under trees, where I could lie down and read. That's where I met Lucía.

'What're you doing?'

It was morning break, and I'd gone to the stands by the netball courts. I was holding a book right in front of me, which made Lucía's question really dumb.

'Reading,' I said.

Apart from an unfortunate-looking Korean girl who joined the school in the ninth grade and left in the tenth, and a girl called Susy del Río, who arrived in the sixth grade and left in the eighth, Lucía had never had any long-term friends. Especially after what happened with Susy del Río: she missed a couple of days of classes, and when the teachers called her house, they were told that her family had moved away. She was never seen again. Lucía was questioned about it several times, but she could not shed any light on her disappearance.

'The Virgin told me that Susy del Río died,' said Karina at the time, fuelling gossip that reached the ears of the headmistress. They called Karina in to explain where she had heard that, and she swore on the lives of her parents and her two little brothers that the Virgin had told her. Not even the headmistress was able to call Karina crazy; in fact, they encouraged her: 'What else did she tell you?' But Karina claimed she had a splitting headache and they sent her to the school nurse. Dalia and I went with her, and there she told us that the Virgin had said more things about Susy del Río, but she didn't want to reveal them out of respect for the dead. According to Karina – or according to the Virgin – Susy del Río had bled to death on a filthy gurney, because her mother had taken her to a black woman in La Boquilla to get an abortion. 'And whose baby was it?' Dalia asked her. Karina shook her head, blinking slowly. 'That's all she said.'

During our first ever chat down by the netball courts, Lucía talked to me about Mauricio. She told me he went to the public university and he really liked it; that he had got onto an Engineering course with really good marks.

'Which university are you going to go to?' I asked her.

'I don't know.'

She bunched up her skirt between her legs. Then she leaned back on her elbows, looked at the sky and it was as if by looking at the clouds, she was able to talk more freely. She talked about the career advice tests – the results of which were far too vague to help you make a decision – and about the school psychologist who was called Jasmine

– 'like a bloody Cocker Spaniel' – and who was over thirty and single, the 'poor thing'.

'…she's one of those ones that can't get married', she went on, 'a numerary, a supernumerary, I can't quite remember.'

'Numerary,' I said.

'Oh yeah, the supers are the ones who get married and give birth endlessly until they finally dry up.'

'Uh-huh.'

'Because they aren't allowed to take the Pill.'

'Yeah.'

'Like Olga Luz.'

Where was she going with this? I carried on with my reading, but then the bell went for the end of break. Lucía sat up.

'I'm going to a birthday party tonight with my boyfriend,' she said.

What had that got to do with me?

'Okay,' I said.

I stood up and dusted down my uniform.

'It's at the Yacht Club. Do you know it?'

I shrugged. 'I've seen it from the outside.'

'Don't you want to come?'

'No.'

'Why not?'

'Because I don't.'

I walked to the classroom at a fast pace. Lucía trailed behind. Before we went into the building, I saw Dalia lying under a tree; she had headphones on and was using her schoolbag as a pillow.

It was too late to back out.

There I was: sitting looking out at the bay, with a glass of beer in my hand and the humid breeze buffing my cheeks. I had dressed as if I couldn't give a flying fuck about the party or the people there, which meant I had spent hours trying on different outfits in front of the mirror. Lucía had not arrived yet, I guessed her boyfriend hadn't either, so I went straight to the bar, grabbed the first drink I saw and headed for the quayside.

'The boats have a really hypnotic effect.' A boy had come and stood next to me.

'The boats or the beer?' I said and he laughed.

There was no denying that it was an incredible view: the lights of the buildings on the opposite shore framed the dark, still water with the moon reflected in it. But the smell was unbearable: the bay was stagnant water, and it smelled like it. And there were mosquitoes the size of cherry stones. I had just shooed one away, when my new friend suggested we move over to a table. He held out his hand to help me up and we went to sit on the terrace. I asked him what he was doing with his life, if he was studying, and if so, what. And then he started using words like hull, and starboard, and porthole, to try and show off his pointless knowledge of boats.

'You don't give a shit about anything I'm saying, do you?' he said. I shook my head and we both laughed. I'd only had half a glass of beer, not enough alcohol to account for how cute I was finding this boy.

'Nobody likes boats until they sail them. One day I'll take you out sailing,' he announced.

And I travelled far, with him, in a boat that set sail from that very spot and crossed the Atlantic on a fast diagonal line to Portugal. On the long journey, we fell out three times and made up six. We had two children: a boy and a girl. And we stopped off at an island to buy them exotic birds, but we couldn't take them with us, because somebody told us that they wouldn't survive outside of the jungle.

'There you are!' Lucía had appeared. She sat down on his lap and kissed him on the lips, and her straightened hair slid across, forming an iron curtain in front of their faces. Next thing I knew, burning rocks came raining down on our boat, just a few miles off Cadiz. We exploded into a gazillion pieces that momentarily blinded me, and then vanished into thin air, like a foolish hope.

5

The Silent Scream

Olga Luz had decided to combine her two weekly classes into just one. Now it was three hours long with a break in the middle. One day she dedicated the whole three hours to abortion; we had to watch a film and discuss it. *Teen Aid* loved those films: the head of a foetus crushed by an enormous pair of forceps or burned by the effect of a syringe that spurted acid after it'd been shoved up the vagina. Babies came out disfigured, but whole; they put them in black bags and then straight in the rubbish.

Every time they showed us one of those films, there would be one girl who would feel sick and would have to run out and throw up. In those days it was better not to even walk past the toilets because they were absolutely filthy: no amount of cleaning product could mask the smell. The films about abortion must have been the symbolic equivalent of the Hieronymus Bosch paintings we'd studied in art class years earlier. The dead foetus and the rotten belly were, like Hell, invariably the consequence of sleeping with a boy. However, you couldn't help thinking how little faith the catechists had in chastity. Their message was clear-cut: you must be chaste. But devoting the next lesson to abortion was like admitting they had failed.

What this revealed was that sex was a redeemable sin; which is why trying to persuade girls not to do it was stupid. A redeemable sin, God knew full well, was the proven method used by many to become Saints. There is nothing more profitable to a religion than a repentant sinner. With chaste girls, it was the same: one day the miserable creature sins and sleeps with someone, gets pregnant, feels guilty and then gets married. From then on, she leads an impeccable life: the sin of sex is redeemed by entering into a life of holy matrimony.

'Break time,' said Lucía.

'Okay,' I replied, but I stayed where I was sitting, watching the classroom emptying of girls, and filling up with light: fragments of afternoon that filtered in through the window and wound their way among the desks until they landed on Olga Luz, who sat curved like a meat hook over her notebook.

'Aren't you coming?' Lucía was about to leave the classroom. I didn't really know why: once we got outside she would just say she was tired and sit on the ground to inspect her cuticles. Then she'd start on about Mauricio this, Mauricio that, and if you tried to change the subject even remotely, she would fall silent, as if someone had switched off her brain.

'No.'

'Want me to stay with you?'

'No.'

'You feeling alright?'

Lucía sapped my energy.

I laid my arms on the desk, leaned my body forward and closed my eyes. There was a moment of silence after that.

'Hey.'

I felt a light tap on my shoulder: it was Dalia. She no longer had such short hair, but it wasn't very long either, so she had pulled it back into messy buns, with rogue hairs bursting out wildly at all angles.

I sat up. She sat down at the desk next to mine, the one

Lucía had been using since Dalia and I had fallen out.

'Will Miss Goody Two-Shoes mind if I sit in her place?

I snorted. 'Don't even think about getting up, please, I'm so sick of her.'

'Oh really? I thought she was your girlfriend.'

Making sure that Olga Luz was not looking, I stuck my middle finger straight up at her, in a perfect *Fuck you*.

The film was called *The Silent Scream* and it was Olga Luz's favourite. It was all about one Mr Bernard Nathanson, an abortion-doctor-turned-Catholic-convert, trying to convince the world that the foetus cried for help before it was killed, in other words, it could sense danger and feel pain. Or in other words, that it was a person. Then they showed the filming of an abortion where the foetus tried to dodge the forceps, the syringe, and when the acid hit it, was seen squirming like an insect doused in bleach. At one point, the camera zoomed in on the face of the foetus, a real close-up shot, and you could see its mouth opening and closing in a desperate gesture that Doctor Nathanson claimed was the word 'mama'. During this part, Olga Luz's nose would stream, and she shuddered as if she had received an electric shock up her ass. Once, in the middle of one of these spasms of anguish, she said that the worst thing about it was that these children would never see the face of God. Because by killing them before they were born, they would be left floating around in a limbo land of deformed babies screaming for their mothers.

It would be years before I fully understood her reaction.

The disturbed behaviour of the Opus Dei teachers was not just because they got off on instilling fear in their pupils, but also because they truly believed what they were saying.

They weren't acting, they really experienced the suffering. Bernard Nathanson must also have believed that the seventy-five thousand abortions or more that he carried out before converting to Catholicism had condemned him to this limbo land of deformed babies. And when he got ill with cancer, he must have thought that he deserved it. In that second before dying – when apparently you see your whole life flash before your eyes – he must have thought that this repentance was not enough to allow him to see the face of God. As a last resort, he must've clung to the hand of his wife Christine, and to divine mercy. Then he would've closed his eyes and let himself fall. In the end, to his relief and misfortune, he would not see his disintegrated particles mixed with the dust, floating in nothingness itself.

That afternoon, Dalia came to pick me up from my grandma's house. We cruised around the city in the truck, listening to "You Oughta Know" by Alanis Morissette, on repeat.

She had fallen out with J.

'Why?'

'Because he's got a girlfriend.'

'Who is she?'

'Some slut from another school.'

'Which one?'

'One where they don't show foetuses dying in agony to their students, so they have no issue spreading their legs for every stud they meet.'

We parked up on a jetty.

Before that, we'd bought ice creams that hadn't lasted long: once they started melting everywhere we'd lobbed them into the sea.

'What about the girls?'

'Which girls?' I had just realised that during those weeks I had not only drifted apart from Dalia, but also from Marcela and Karina. We were one of those groups that needed a core to stay together, and if that core broke apart, the group vanished. That made me sad. Suddenly I missed Karina's horrible obsession with inspecting your face with her huge round eyes, in a kind of trance, trying to spot blackheads emerging from your skin.

'I think Marcela's going to do an exchange in Boston,' said Dalia. But it sounded like she'd just made that up. Then she stretched her legs out and I saw that she had shaved. Too much time had passed between us.

'And Lucía?' she said.

'What about Lucía?'

'How did she go from being part of the furniture, to being your pet?'

'For God's sake, what do you mean…'

'Is she still with that boyfriend?'

'Which boyfriend?'

'The dumbass one.'

I didn't answer. If I did, she would argue with me.

If I argued, I lost.

A couple of nights before, Mauricio had called me on the phone. We talked about nothing in particular: hi, how are you? / good, you? / good / that's good / yeah, that's good. Neither of us mentioned Lucía. We ended up in silence, almost asleep, which was a great achievement in my case, seeing as the phone was in the most uncomfortable little corner of my grandma's living room, cluttered with figurines of saints and crucifixes. And just as we reached the climax of the conversation – that is, the only full sentence of the evening – a dry cough erupted in the air. 'Decent girls don't talk at this time of night.' It was my grandma – or an apparition of her — swathed in her translucent dressing gown. Through it you could see her body, a suit made of creases, and saggy leathery skin. Layer upon layer of sad skin.

'A complete and utter dumbass, that's what they say about that guy.' Dalia was looking at the horizon, while I sat there feeling humiliated. I followed her gaze: the sun was a fistful of fire, about to be extinguished.

I was hungry. I wanted to go back to my grandma's house and eat some re-heated leftovers and then lie down on my bed and look at the cracks in the ceiling until I fell asleep. What a pointless day, I thought.

Every so often, fragments of *The Silent Scream* flashed through my head.

'So, is he a dumbass, or not?' she insisted.

'Who?' She had managed to piss me off.

'That Mauricio guy, the one who's going out with that bitch Lucía.'

I sighed, exasperated.

'I don't know, Dalia, he doesn't seem like one to me.'

She burst out laughing.

'I knew it.'

'You knew what?'

'That you like Lucía's boyfriend.'

'You're crazy,' I said. 'Crazy and full of shit.'

Dalia's laughter really shook me up. It wasn't a feeling of anger, it was more like a blade slowly being plunged into my chest. I stood up and walked to the street. I dried my tears on the sleeve of my shirt. When I looked up to carry on walking, it was night time.

Mauricio came in a taxi.

I was still sitting next to the phone box. I was watching

the waves brimming with foam, furiously raging. I had just seen a boat coming in on the horizon. It was as big as a whale and must have had hundreds of tourists on board, cooped up like dogs in kennels.

Mauricio sat down next to me and didn't mention my puffy eyes. After a while, he stood up and held out his hand.

'Let's walk.'

That seemed like a good idea, it was too hot to be sitting there, melting. We crossed over to the beach and there was a guy with a cool box full of beers. Mauricio bought two. He took off his shoes, rolled up the bottoms of his jeans. I did the same. We passed by a shrimp and ceviche stand that was closing, a guy was sweeping up the shrimp shells scattered all over the sand, and piling them up behind a tin tank. We sat down. Mauricio opened a beer and passed it to me. I didn't want it. He asked me what I wanted.

'How do you mean, what do I want?'

'A Coke, a lemonade… I can go and get you one.'

I looked around. Everything was closed.

'I don't want anything,' I said.

'Nothing at all?'

'No.'

But it was clear that I did.

Mauricio put his arm around my waist, pulled me in and kissed my cheek. I turned my back on him. He hugged me from behind and drew me in close to him. We were in such a close embrace that I could feel his breath on the back of my neck. He moved his hands up and touched my breasts, which were tiny, compared to Lucía's. I pulled away again. But he persisted, this time he moved in front of me and kissed me on the lips. Seconds later, we were lying on the sand, feeling each other up under our clothes like a couple of dirty hippies.

'On your feet, ladies and gents.'

A policeman was shining a torch on us.

We jumped to our feet, and I turned my back because I was embarrassed. I shook the sand out of my hair. Mauricio apologised to the man, who was pretending to be cross, but in the middle he laughed and made sexist jokes.

'Very well, I understand young man, but do me a favour, be a gentleman and take the young lady to a hotel.'

'Yes, sir.'

'This is a tourist city, it's full of hotels. Didn't you see that one?'

I presumed he was pointing at the Hotel Caribe. Mauricio couldn't have afforded a room there in a million years.

'Yes, sir.'

'And if that one isn't to your liking, I'd recommend this one.'

Out of the corner of my eye I saw him hand Mauricio a card. I was sure it was some filthy motel where he and his colleagues took housemaids. I felt horrible.

'Okay, buddy,' said the policeman, nodding vigorously, 'you two have fun.'

The way back was even more humiliating: we sat far apart in the back seat of the taxi, not touching. A provincial *vallenato* was playing on the radio, it was about a woman with tiny, bewitching peasant's eyes that sparkled like sapphires. I felt suffocated; something large, rough and alive was obstructing my throat.

I had nowhere to go, nobody waiting me for anywhere. Mauricio did.

As we crossed the bridge back into Manga I looked out of the window; the lighthouse in the bay cast out a beam of light that was swallowed up by the darkness, as if by the cavernous mouth of a wolf.

6

The Morning After

I didn't like Father Tiago because when he gave you communion bread he touched your tongue with his thumb. This meant that you ended up swallowing, along with the body of Christ, the saliva of everyone who went up to take communion. Luckily, his masses were last thing on a Friday, so from there you could go straight home to gargle with mouthwash. Father Tiago was not a permanent priest at the chapel, he only came in for special occasions. The special occasion in this case was that we were about to graduate and, although he would be doing the mass for the ceremony, today would be the last time at school.

After mass, the headmistress came to our classroom. We thought she would give us one of those talks about what awaited us on the outside, in the real world, where we should always remember that we were nothing more than an instrument of Our Lord God, 'We are the clay, and He the potter' – she would say, half-closing her eyes as if dazzled by a bright light. Everything that happened to us was part of His plan for us. 'Then why bother getting out of bed in the morning?' Marcela had asked once, mortified by the idea of being a puppet. The weirdest thing was that, after fifteen years of Catholic school education, she had only just realised this. The headmistress told her, 'to please Him.'

But today she hadn't come to talk about that. Or not exactly.

'A tragedy has occurred.'

The headmistress had big teeth. This meant that she could never close her mouth properly.

A girl in ninth grade had been admitted to hospital, with an uncertain prognosis:

'... in the hands of God.'

Her parents were sleeping, they heard the doorbell and when they went to the door they found her, unconscious and with her clothing torn. They heard the screech of car tyres disappearing around the corner.

'Whatever happens, we must accept His will.'

The girl had gone to a *quinceañera* party at a nightclub hired out for the occasion. At the venue, there was a specially designated mezzanine area for the parents. The girls and boys were on the ground floor, circling the European DJ and the drinks table. 'They were soft cocktails,' the mother of the birthday girl said later. It must have been true. According to the abridged versions, a group of bad boys who nobody wanted to name (it was a tiny city, we all knew who the bad boys were) had put Rohypnol in her drink. Then they took her out for a drive, parked up at a jetty, took their shoes off, strolled along the beach in their fancy suits.

Up to that point: an advert for mentholated chewing gum.

Up to that point: the start of an N Sync video.

Up to that point: a bunch of posing gayboys.

But there was a gap in the middle that none of the versions could fill in. All we knew was that the girl had appeared, dumped on her own doorstep, having been beaten up and raped. They found seven types of semen in her, and not just in the front.

Yet all of this was incidental. For the headmistress – and that was why she had come to pay us a visit – the real dilemma was whether to expel her now, all damaged, or to wait for her hopefully speedy recovery, and then do it. Either way, she would have to be expelled, and not because of what had happened to her, poor thing, but because of how, blinded by pain, and tempted by the devil, her parents had acted.

That must have been the first time I heard of the morning-after pill. The year was 1997, and I had never heard of that pill, which had been in use for nearly thirty years. I remember that I was sitting at the back of the classroom, with my headphones hidden inside my blazer: *Oh no, I know a dirty word*, Kurt was whispering in my right ear. The left ear was listening attentively to the headmistress, who was announcing the apocalypse, because the unknown potential of a creature with seven fathers had been snuffed out.

In the afternoon I felt feverish.

I slept so long that when I woke up, night was gnawing at my window.

Outside, I could hear the voices of my grandma and the maid, embroiled in some domestic discussion. I went out. The house stank of onion and boiled fish. The maid was trying to convince my grandma to please let her finish her work. That woman was a saint: eight in the evening and she was still there, dealing with an old woman coughing her bad breath in her face. I carried on until I got to the dining room window that looked out onto the street. I leaned out. Some carts were going past, on the way back from the market, full of rotten stuff they'd been unable to sell. A fog surrounded them, but it wasn't fog. It was the dirt that had been stuck to the pavement, which at that time of night was whipped up by the breeze.

I thought about Mauricio.

Nothing new there: I was always thinking about Mauricio.

I imagined him with Lucía, licking her like a dog. I imagined him raping the girl in ninth grade. And with Father Tiago, receiving communion, chewing off his fingers, his hand, devouring his whole arm as he let out a carnal, cannibalistic groan. He'd called me every day lately, but I had given the maid instructions. I'd written a series of responses on the message pad: the girl doesn't live here anymore / no, she didn't leave a phone number / I think the girl moved to Houston / yes, Houston, she's about to board a space shuttle, destination unknown. But she never managed to get to the last two sentences, she would get flustered and hang up nervously.

My grandma huffed out of the kitchen and started shuffling towards her bedroom, but then she stopped in her tracks.

'Grandma?'

She did not reply. I got up from the dining table and went over to her, and took her by the shoulders:

'Grandma, are you okay?'

She looked at me as if she didn't recognise me. Her eyes were watery, and she had eye gunk crusted in the corners. I was used to her sickly appearance and her sudden disorientation, but this time, she also looked creased and dirty, like an old pillowcase. My grandma was short, with very pale, paper-thin skin and eyes a faded brown colour. And when she didn't brush her hair, the hairs around her forehead formed a grey crown that made her look sad and unkempt. She made a rasping sound when she breathed, as if she had calluses in her airways.

'Am I okay?' she asked me.

I felt trapped by her question: I had the sensation that this frail old woman I was holding by the shoulders was not her, but me. And her face was a mirror.

Stray hairs.

That's what they called those dark, wiry hairs that grew out of the skull, sharp and erect, as a sign of rebellion compared to the docility of the others. At a certain time of day, generally the dead time between the last period and the end of school, a row of girls could be seen in front of the mirror in the toilets, plucking out those stray hairs and depositing them on the countertop. In the end, there were scattered heaps of hair left, which the cleaning lady would collect up in a bag. Genetic material thrown in the rubbish.

Marcela, Karina and I were doing this when Lucía showed up. She came over to us like a small, timorous animal, and leaned her back against the wall. I looked at her from the mirror and said, 'What's up?' She shook her head, to say not a lot, she was just watching.

Then she said, 'Poor Dianita, what do you think will happen to her?'

'Who is Dianita?' asked Marcela.

I had been grappling with a hair that I couldn't quite manage to pull out by the root, and each time the hair was just getting shorter and shorter, and more difficult to pull out. I had had enough of looking for stray hairs and I sat down on the side by the sinks. Karina had moved on to plucking her eyebrows. I thought it was sad, but above all pointless, our obsession with eradicating our hair. They said that every time you removed a hair, the root got stronger and another even tougher one started to grow. We were fighting a losing battle of the will against nature. And when it came down to it, who really cared about our hairs? Girls. Men would never look at us scrupulously as we did ourselves.

'The girl in ninth grade,' replied Lucía, slightly taken aback by the fact that Marcela didn't know the girl's name.

I didn't know her name either. Karina did, because she was a total gossip.

That morning, the parents of the raped girl showed up at the headmistress's office. They emerged all tearful. Apparently, they were holding an envelope containing a piece of paper with the names and surnames of the rapists on it.

'Everyone knows what will happen,' said Karina.

The parents did not report it to the police, they didn't even talk to the parents of the rapists, but they decided to apply a punishment that was about right for that city: expelling them. They went, with said envelope, to the boys' school (which was the same as ours, but for boys), to the local parish church, and to the newspaper, where nothing would be printed because the editor was a relation of one of the boys. Most likely, all that would happen is that the boys would be sent abroad for a while. Then they'd come back, go off to study some second-rate degree course at a university in Bogotá, before returning to Cartagena to run their parents' businesses, get married and have children who they'd name after themselves, and who would appear on the social announcements pages when they got baptised, when they took their first communion, when they got confirmed, when they graduated, and when they got married to some bilingual girl who talked to the Virgin, with her hymen intact, but her ass in tatters.

For Dianita it would be a very different story. For the moment, she would stay here, wandering the city, looking for a half-decent school to take her in – it was not easy to get accepted by a decent school if you'd been expelled from somewhere else.

'It's so awful,' Lucía put her hands to her face.

For a very brief moment I saw us grown. Not grown up, but grown: adult, slightly old and pitiful, at the bottom of a well that I could peer down, shining a torch. I glimpsed into the future. A future that looked dull, bland, and dark. I tried to imagine us different; transformed into something else.

Atheist. Nympho. Lesbian. Adulterous. Wild.

Or sane.

I wasn't able to.

Just then Dalia came in. He eyes were red, her pupils slightly enlarged. She was carrying the Snoopy thermos under her arm.

'What are you lot up to?' she said. 'I've been looking for you.'

She had rum breath and her uniform was dishevelled.

Karina looked her up and down with that indignant face, the one that made you want to throw acid over it, to erase it.

'We were talking about Dianita,' said Lucía. 'So awful.'

'Who?' said Dalia, but she didn't wait for a reply. She just laughed and said, nodding in my direction, 'Did she tell you yet?'

'Huh?' stammered Lucía.

'Did she tell you that your boyfriend licked out her…'

I reacted just in time, stretching out my leg and kicking her in the cheekbone. She cried out, stumbled. The thermos flask rolled onto the floor. Dalia bent down to get it and fell over, howling with drunken laughter. Karina and Marcela ran over to help her. Lucía stayed where she was, still and quiet: a pale, expressionless mummy.

'You're disgusting,' I said to Dalia, as she laughed on the floor, writhing around like a worm on the dirty tiles. I kicked her again, this time in the ribs, and I would have carried on kicking, if Marcela hadn't bundled me out of the toilets.

'Are you okay?' she asked, once we were outside. Her eyes shone with nervous energy.

We sat on the ground, by the school exit: waves of pupils were trooping towards the car park and getting on buses, finding their seats, primping their hair, wiping the sweat from their top lips with a tissue. That, I thought, is what limbo must be like. All of them marching to the shared rhythm of an internal music that only existed there; that they would be incapable of reproducing on the outside.

I felt the sun beating down on my forehead, clouding my vision.

I felt thirsty and tired.

Marcela tucked my sweaty hair behind my ear.

'Am I okay?' I asked her. I was panting.

She just shook her head.

TRANSLATOR'S NOTE

There is a widely held belief that a perfectly pitched translation can only be achieved if the translator has first-hand experience of the country where the book is set, or where the author is from, and in-depth knowledge of the cultural and political background of that country and its linguistic idiosyncrasies. When I first read *Waiting for a Hurricane*, *Worse Things*, and *Sexual Education*, which we brought together in the volume you have here, *Fish Soup*, I knew very little about Margarita García Robayo, other than her age and where she's from. And I should make a little confession: Colombia is still on my list of countries to visit. I thought there would be so many 'Colombianisms' in her writing that I wouldn't know, and references that might be lost on me. I thought we would be so different, she and I – one of us from the hot, salty, coastal city of Cartagena, and the other from a cathedral city amid the damp, green fields of Wiltshire. As I set about translating, I did feel a sense of trepidation.

I needn't have worried. There is something so universal about Margarita's writing. She shows us a different side to the Caribbean coast of Colombia. It is not the sunny, sandy, picture-perfect postcard image we might have in our heads. Neither does she reveal the grimy, criminal underbelly of violence and drug lords. Her characters and stories simply revolve around the ones in the 'middle': the ordinary people trying to get somewhere in life without losing their minds, their jobs, their health, their loved ones.

During that first reading, she had me laughing, and even welling up. I instantly started seeking out the words in my head, thinking how to go about writing it in English. For a translator that is the best sign. It meant I had found her voice. Or it had found me. So easily, in fact, that at times I worried about appropriating the text, putting too much of my own 'stamp' on it, and making it less 'hers'– something many translators feel at times. I was instantly connected to her world. Because, really, her world is not that different from mine. I completely understood her fascination with migration, with the desire to escape, with families, her obsession with crumbling relationships, with people trying to hold it together and appear normal while they are falling apart. She is the queen of unhappy endings. Yet she is far from depressing to read. She manages to create hope without sentimentality, and the beauty of her writing lies in the tough situations she shrewdly crafts. Her characters keep on keeping on, because life is about survival. I delighted in the surreal element of her writing, the crazy, visceral dreams, the descriptions of sex and bodily functions. There is a filthiness to her prose. She is blunt and brave, saying the things we all think but would never dare to say. She observes, she subverts. All of these elements spoke to me.

You may not like her characters, and that is precisely because they are real. In them, we see the bare bones of what it means to be human, and we are forced to admit that we are flawed too. Some people might find it hard to swallow this truth about the banality of life, sex and relation-ships. Not me. I gulped her prose down hungrily, savouring the controlled, detached way she is able to depict utter despair; relishing the cynicism, the flashes of dark humour. The way she expresses the thoughts we all have, no matter how disgusting or how wrong. I gulped it all down, and back out it came, transformed and yet the same, sometimes needing a twist or a tweak, a touch of my own. Something I felt she would appreciate. What I found in Margarita's writing was everything I hoped I could have written if, in an alternate life, I was a thirty-something author from Colombia. Everything I observe and feel in my own life is there, in her narrative. I wish I could have written this book. Which is fortunate because, in a way, I've had the chance to do exactly that.

The pressure of finding an author's 'voice' and doing their work 'justice' constantly weighs on a translator. All you can ever hope for is that you convey what the author intended, without losing the author from their own text – somehow managing to capture the poetry, the rhythm, the cadence, the soul of the original. Margarita admitted that she felt a similar trepidation about being translated into English: 'As a writer, I work very hard at trying to give every story a kind of rhythm, a music. I didn't know if that was possible to translate. But Charlotte did it in a fabulous way. When I read some of the fragments that she sent me, I was able to recognise *me* in there, and that was unbelievable, really amazing.'

I couldn't ask for more than that.

I'd like to thank Carolina at Charco Press, for all her support and for the endless conversations about bottoms, bums, arses, asses, butts, and other body parts. And my talented editor Fionn Petch, for helping me to shape this text into its current form. And of course, Margarita García Robayo, for writing all the things I wish I could have written.

Charlotte Coombe

CHARCO PRESS

Director/Editor: Carolina Orloff
Director: Samuel McDowell

www.charcopress.com

Fish Soup was published on
80gsm Munken Print Cream paper.

The text was designed using Bembo 11 and ITC Galliard Pro.

Printed in July 2019 by TJ International
Padstow, Cornwall, PL28 8RW using responsibly sourced paper
and environmentally-friendly adhesive.